Invisible Ink

English translations of works by Patrick Modiano

From Yale University Press
After the Circus
Family Record
Invisible Ink
Little Jewel
Paris Nocturne
Pedigree: A Memoir
Sleep of Memory
Such Fine Boys
Sundays in August
*Suspended Sentences: Three Novellas (Afterimage, Suspended
    Sentences,* and *Flowers of Ruin)*

Also available
The Black Notebook
Catherine Certitude
Dora Bruder
Honeymoon
In the Café of Lost Youth
Lacombe Lucien
Missing Person
The Occupation Trilogy (The Night Watch, Ring Roads, and
    La Place de l'Etoile)
Out of the Dark
So You Don't Get Lost in the Neighborhood
28 Paradises (with Dominique Zehrfuss)
Villa Triste
Young Once

Invisible Ink

A Novel

Patrick Modiano

*Translated from the French
by Mark Polizzotti*

Yale UNIVERSITY PRESS · NEW HAVEN AND LONDON

A MARGELLOS
WORLD REPUBLIC OF LETTERS BOOK

The Margellos World Republic of Letters is dedicated to making literary works from around the globe available in English through translation. It brings to the English-speaking world the work of leading poets, novelists, essayists, philosophers, and playwrights from Europe, Latin America, Africa, Asia, and the Middle East to stimulate international discourse and creative exchange.

Yale University Press books may be purchased in quantity for educational, business, or promotional use. For information, please e-mail sales.press@yale.edu (U.S. office) or sales@yaleup.co.uk (U.K. office).

Set in Baskerville type by Tseng Information Systems, Inc.
Printed in the United States of America.

Library of Congress Control Number: 2020935048
ISBN 978-0-300-25258-3 (hardcover : alk. paper)

A catalogue record for this book is available from the British Library.
This paper meets the requirements of ANSI/NISO z39.48-1992 (Permanence of Paper).

10 9 8 7 6 5 4 3 2 1

Whoever wants to remember himself
must entrust himself to forgetfulness,
to the risk that absolute forgetfulness is,
and to the beautiful chance that memory
then becomes.
—Maurice Blanchot

Invisible Ink

There are blanks in this life, white spaces you can detect if you open the "case file": a single sheet in a sky-blue folder that has faded with time. That ancient sky blue has itself turned almost white. And the words "case file" are written across the middle of the folder. In black ink.

This is my only remnant of the Hutte Detective Agency, the only trace of my passage in that old three-room apartment whose windows looked out on a courtyard. I was no more than twenty. Hutte's office occupied the room in back, along with a cabinet in which he stored the archives. Why this file rather than another? No doubt because of the blanks. And besides, it wasn't in the cabinet, but sitting abandoned on Hutte's desk. A "case," as he called it, that hadn't yet been solved—would it ever be?— and the first one he talked about on the evening when he'd hired me "on a trial basis," to use his expression. A few months later, on another evening at the same hour, when I had given up this job and left the Hutte Agency for good, I had, unbeknownst to Hutte and after saying my good-byes, slid into my briefcase the fact sheet in its sky-blue folder that was lying on his desk. As a souvenir.

Yes, my first assignment from Hutte was related to that fact sheet. I was to ask the concierge of an apartment building in the 15th arrondissement whether she'd heard from a certain Noëlle Lefebvre, a person who posed a dual problem for Hutte: not only had she suddenly disappeared, but we weren't certain of her true identity. After seeing the concierge, Hutte instructed, I was to go to a branch of the post office, with a card he'd given me. On it was Noëlle Lefebvre's name, address, and photo, and it was used for retrieving mail at the General Delivery window. The aforesaid Noëlle Lefebvre had left it behind. After that, I should go to a particular café to ask if anyone had seen Noëlle Lefebvre lately, sit at a table, and stay there for the rest of the afternoon, in case Noëlle Lefebvre showed up. All this in the same neighborhood and on the same day.

The concierge at the apartment house took a long time to answer. I knocked more and more insistently on the glass door of her lodge. The door opened onto a drowsy face. At first, it seemed like the name Noëlle Lefebvre meant nothing to her.

"Have you seen her lately?"

Finally, in a curt voice: "No, sir . . . I haven't seen her in over a month."

I didn't dare ask anything further. I wouldn't have had time, as she immediately slammed the door.

At the General Delivery window, the man scrutinized the card I'd handed him.

"But, sir, you're not Noëlle Lefebvre."

"She's away from Paris," I told him. "She asked me to pick up her mail."

At that, he got up and walked to a row of

pigeonholes. He examined the few letters they contained. He came back toward me, shaking his head.

"Nothing addressed to Noëlle Lefebvre."

The only remaining step was to go to the café Hutte had mentioned.

An early afternoon. No one in the small interior, except one man, behind the bar, face buried in a newspaper. He didn't see me come in and continued reading. I didn't know exactly how to formulate my question. Simply hand him the General Delivery card in Noëlle Lefebvre's name? I was embarrassed by the role Hutte was making me play, which clashed with my natural shyness. He raised his eyes.

"You wouldn't have seen Noëlle Lefebvre lately, would you?"

I felt like I was speaking too fast, so fast that I mumbled.

"Noëlle? No."

He had answered so briefly that I was tempted to ask more questions about the woman. But I was afraid of rousing his suspicions. I sat at one of the tables on the small terrace that spilled out onto the sidewalk. He came to take my order. It was the opportunity to try and find out more. Innocuous phrases crowded into my head, which might have elicited concrete answers.

"I think I'll just wait for her . . . You never know with Noëlle . . . Do you think she's still living in the neighborhood? . . . Wouldn't you know, she said she'd meet me here . . . Have you known her long?"

But when he served my grenadine, I said nothing.

I took out the card Hutte had lent me. And now that we're in the next century, I've stopped writing for a moment on page 7 of this Clairefontaine writing pad to have another look at that card, which lives in the file. "The bearer is authorized to receive General Delivery correspondence without surcharge. Authorization no. 1. Last name: Lefebvre. First name: Noëlle. Address: Paris 15. Number and street: 88 Convention. Cardholder's photograph. Is authorized to

receive, without surcharge, correspondence addressed to bearer c/o General Delivery."

The photo is much larger than a simple
photo booth picture. And too dark. You can't tell
the color of her eyes. Or her hair: brown? light
chestnut? On the café terrace that afternoon, I
stared as intently as I could at that face whose
features I could barely distinguish, and I wasn't
sure I'd be able to recognize Noëlle Lefebvre.

I remember it was early spring. The small
terrace was in the sun and now and again the
sky clouded over. An awning above the terrace
protected me from rain showers. When a silhouette who might have been Noëlle Lefebvre came
down the sidewalk, I followed her with my gaze,
waiting to see whether she entered the café. Why
hadn't Hutte given me more clues about how
to approach her? "You'll figure it out. Shadow
her so I know if she's still hanging around the
area." The expression "shadow her" had made
me laugh. And Hutte had looked on in silence,
brows knit, as if dismayed by my frivolity.

The afternoon passed slowly, and I was still sitting at a table on the terrace. I imagined the paths Noëlle Lefebvre might follow from her building to the post office, from the post office to the café. No doubt she also frequented other places in the neighborhood: a movie theater, some shops . . . Two or three people she often saw in the street could have vouched for her existence. Or a single person with whom she shared her life.

I resolved to check at General Delivery every day. Sooner or later, a letter would have to fall into my hands, one of those letters that never reach their destination. No forwarding address. Or else, I'd stay in the neighborhood for a while. I'd get myself a room. I'd pace the area between her building, the post office, and the café, and I would enlarge my field of observation in concentric circles. I'd stay attentive to people's comings and goings on the streets and get to know their faces, like someone watching for the oscillations of a pendulum, poised to detect the tiniest waves. All I needed was a little patience, and in that period of my life, I felt capable of waiting for hours in the sun and rain.

A few customers had entered the café, but I hadn't recognized Noëlle Lefebvre among them. I watched them through the window behind me. They were sitting at tables—except for one, who was standing at the bar and talking to the owner. I had spotted him as soon as he came in. He must have been around my age, in any case no more than twenty-five. He was tall, with dark hair, wearing a sheepskin jacket. The owner pointed me out almost imperceptibly, and the other trained his eyes on me. But with the window between us, it was easy for me, by turning my head slightly, to make it appear I hadn't noticed.

"Sir, a moment, please . . . Sir . . ."

I sometimes hear those words in my dreams, spoken in a tone of affected gentleness, but with menace showing through. It was the young man in the sheepskin jacket. I pretended not to hear.

"A moment, please . . . Sir . . ."

His tone had become sharper, like someone catching you red-handed. I looked up at him.

"Sir . . ."

I was taken aback by his use of the term "sir," even though we were the same age. His features were tense, and I sensed he distrusted me. I gave him a broad smile, but my smile seemed only to exasperate him.

"They say you're looking for Noëlle . . ."

He stood there, by my table, as if trying to provoke me.

"Yes. Perhaps you could tell me what she's up to . . ."

"For what reason?" he asked in a haughty tone.

I felt like standing up and ditching him then and there.

"What reason? She's a friend, that's all. She asked me to pick up her mail at the post office."

I showed him the card with Noëlle Lefebvre's photo stapled to it.

"Do you recognize her?"

He studied the picture. Then he reached out as if to snatch the card away, but I jerked it back.

He finally sat down at my table, or rather let himself drop onto the wicker chair. I could tell he'd started taking me seriously.

"I don't understand . . . You were supposed to pick up her mail?"

"Yes. In a post office a bit farther up the street, on Rue de la Convention."

"Did Roger know about this?"

"Roger? Who's Roger?"

"Don't you know her husband?"

"No."

I wondered whether I'd read the fact sheet in Hutte's office too quickly—a very brief write-up, barely three paragraphs long. Yet I was fairly certain it hadn't mentioned Noëlle Lefebvre being married.

"You mean Roger Lefebvre?" I asked.

He shrugged.

"Hardly. Her husband's name is Roger Be-haviour . . . And who are you, exactly?"

He had brought his face close to mine and was fixing me with an insolent stare.

"A friend of Noëlle Lefebvre's. I knew her by her maiden name . . ."

I had said this in such a calm voice that he softened a bit.

"It's funny, I never saw you with Noëlle . . ."

"My name is Eyben. Jean Eyben. I met Noëlle Lefebvre a few months ago. She never said she was married."

He kept silent and looked distraught.

"She asked me to go pick up her mail at General Delivery. I thought maybe she'd changed neighborhoods."

"No, she didn't," he said in a serious voice. "She lived here with Roger. At 13 Rue Vaugelas. I haven't heard from her since."

"And what's your name?"

I immediately regretted having put the question so bluntly.

"Gérard Mourade."

Evidently, Hutte's fact sheet was light on facts. There was no mention of a Gérard Mourade. No more than of a Roger Behaviour, Noëlle Lefebvre's purported husband.

"Noëlle never told you about Roger? Or me? That's kind of strange . . . My name is Gé-rard Mou-rade . . ."

He had repeated his name very loudly, detaching each syllable, as if wishing to convince me of his identity once and for all and awaken a forgotten memory, or rather persuade me how important Gérard Mourade was.

"I get the sense we're not talking about the same person . . ."

I felt like answering, just to reassure him, that he was right and that, all things considered, there must have been a number of Noëlle Lefebvres in France. And we would have parted company on amicable terms.

I'm trying my best to transcribe the dialogue I had that afternoon with Gérard Mourade, but after such a stretch of years only scraps of it remain. I wish the whole thing had been tape-recorded. If so, listening to it today, I wouldn't feel like our conversation took place so far in the past, but rather that it belonged to an eternal present. In the background, for all time, you would have heard the sounds of a spring afternoon on Rue de la Convention, the shouts of children coming home from the school next door — children who by now would be middle-aged. And that waft of the present, having managed to pass intact through nearly half a century, would have let me better understand my state of mind at the time. Hutte had offered me a position in his agency — a very minor position — but I had no desire whatsoever to follow that path. I had thought this temporary job would provide me with all the documentation I needed to inspire me later on if I decided to pursue a literary calling. The school of life, as it were.

He explained to me that he'd received a visit a few weeks before from a "client" whose name figured at the top of the fact sheet: Brainos, 194

Avenue Victor-Hugo. This man had asked him to look into the disappearance of Noëlle Lefebvre. And I, once I found myself at the General Delivery window of the post office, had hoped that a letter or telegram addressed to this Noëlle Lefebvre might set us on her trail. On the café terrace, the more time passed, the more hopeful I grew. I was almost certain she'd appear at any moment.

It was the end of the afternoon. Gérard Mourade was still sitting across from me.

"We're talking about the same person," I said.

I again held out the General Delivery card. He studied it for a long moment.

"That's her, all right. But why Rue de la Convention? She lived with Roger on Rue Vaugelas."

"Could that have been her address before she got married?"

"Roger told me she'd only just arrived in Paris when he met her."

The information Hutte had gathered was vague. He must have jotted it down in haste, like a bad pupil doing his vacation homework.

"But what about you—I'd love to know how you met Noëlle . . ."

He again looked at me warily. I was tempted to tell him the truth, as this cat-and-mouse game was growing tiresome. I searched for the right words: fact sheet . . . detective agency . . . Those words bothered me. Even the name Hutte put me ill at ease, because of a disquieting sound it hadn't had until then. I said nothing. I stopped myself in time. Afterward, I believe I felt the same relief at not having revealed my true face as someone who has climbed over the parapet of a bridge to leap into the void and then changed his mind. Yes, relief. And also a slight feeling of vertigo.

"I met Noëlle Lefebvre a few months ago at this fellow Brainos's place."

It was the name of the man who had come to see Hutte and who wanted to know the reasons behind Noëlle Lefebvre's disappearance. But I hadn't been at the agency that day, and I regretted it. Hutte had not given me any description of the man.

"Do you know Brainos?" I asked him.

"No, I don't. I never heard the name, from Noëlle or from Roger."

He was clearly waiting for me to offer more details, but I knew nothing about the man. And the sheet with his name on it gave only his address: 194 Avenue Victor-Hugo. Would it have been asking too much for Hutte to provide some clarifications about his "client" before sending me out into the field?

I would have to make something up, tell a lie to get at the truth. Of course, I'd always enjoyed slipping into other people's lives, out of curiosity, but also out of a need to understand them better and disentangle the enmeshed strands of their existence — something they were often incapable of doing themselves because they were too close to it, while I had the advantage of being a simple spectator, or rather a witness, as one might say in court.

"Brainos . . . He's a doctor . . . I met Noëlle Lefebvre one afternoon last May in his waiting room . . ."

He knitted his brow, as if he only half-believed me.

I labored to come up with other details that might convince him, but the fact is, that day, the exercise was proving difficult. Had I lost my touch?

"I think she was hoping this Dr. Brainos would write her a prescription . . ."

"A prescription? Whatever for?"

I couldn't answer. Before taking the metro to Javel station, I should have jotted down a few notes, a kind of crib sheet. Don't improvise. "Dr. Brainos" . . . It rang false.

"For anxiety . . . She was worried about her job . . . She needed tranquilizers . . ."

"You really think so? And yet, she'd been re-lieved to get the job at Lancel . . ."

Lancel? Perhaps he meant the luxury leather goods shop on Place de l'Opéra. It was time to take a risk to learn more—to bluff, as poker players said.

"She told me she didn't like the commute to work, every morning and night . . . From her

building to Place de l'Opéra required at least
two transfers in the metro, didn't it?"

He nodded as if in approval. I had guessed
right. And yet, that late afternoon, I no longer
felt up to playing the game. I was at risk of stray-
ing too far off the path from groping so much in
the dark.

"That's true," he said, "she did often com-
plain about the commute to Lancel . . . It's not
very convenient if you live in this neighborhood . . ."

"And what about Roger, what did he do?"

I had asked the question in an offhand voice,
as if it were unimportant. It was a method Hutte
had taught me for getting people to talk. "Otherwise," he'd said, "they might clam up."

"Roger? Oh, a bit of this, a bit of that . . .
When I first met him, he was a driver for a moving company . . . Then he worked at Orève,
a florist in the 16th arrondissement . . . A few
months ago, he got a job as assistant stage manager in a theater company . . . my doing . . ."

Listing Roger's various employments, he seemed to feel a certain admiration for him.

"Roger always landed on his feet . . ."

Apparently, this was an expression he and Roger repeated often, a kind of code word. But scarcely had he uttered it before his smile froze.

"And now, lord knows where he is . . . The last time I saw him, he said he was going to look for Noëlle . . ."

"She disappeared first?" I asked.

"Yes. One evening she didn't come home to Rue Vaugelas. Nor the next day. I went with Roger to Lancel. They didn't know anything about it."

"And you don't have a clue, you or her husband, what could possibly have happened?"

I had chosen a neutral expression, "what could possibly have happened," so that he'd feel free to confide in me or confess something. That was another of Hutte's lessons: don't ask for precise details. Avoid seeming aggressive when questioning someone. "Go lightly."

He appeared to be feeling some hesitation, some embarrassment.

"What exactly do you mean by 'what could possibly have happened'?"

Yes, he was visibly uncomfortable, as if he suspected I knew something. But what? I preferred to respond with a simple shrug. In silence.

"And what about you, what do you do for a living?"

I had adopted a casual tone. I gave him a smile. I sensed I'd aroused his distrust once again, and that he might have been hiding some detail concerning Noëlle Lefebvre, her husband, and himself. Two people don't just disappear so suddenly without someone close to them having ideas about it, however tentative.

"Me? I'm an actor. For the last year I've been taking the Paupelix Course."

"How's that working out?"

No doubt it had been tactless of me to ask such a direct question.

"I get walk-on parts in movies," he said curtly. "It earns enough to pay for the course."

I'd never heard of the Paupelix Course. In the days following, I checked up on it, so that today I can write the name without misspelling: Paupelix, professor of dramatic arts, 37 Rue de l'Arcade, Paris 8. It explained certain facial expressions, certain overly studied poses and gestures that I'd noticed him make, which he must have learned at the Paupelix Course.

"So, then, you used to see Noëlle often? I just can't understand how she never told you about Roger . . ."

Clearly he was trying to find out what kind of relationship had existed between Noëlle Lefebvre and me, and it was making him anxious.

"She did talk about her life, didn't she?"

"Not really," I said. "We only saw each other three or four times . . . in the evening, when she got off work at Lancel . . . At the café across the street, on Boulevard des Capucines . . ."

The fact sheet gave her date and place of birth, but the latter was rather vague: "a village near Annecy, in Haute-Savoie."

"We discovered we were both born in the

same region. Around Annecy. We mostly talked about that."

He seemed not to know that detail of Noëlle Lefebvre's life or to grant it much significance. But I was certain Hutte would have felt the same as I did: it's always important to know in what neighborhood or village people were born.

"And those letters she had you pick up at General Delivery—who could have written them?"

"No idea. On the envelopes, I noticed it was always the same handwriting, in Florida blue ink . . ."

I wondered if it helped to make up that kind of detail. I wished he would give me some more specifics about Noëlle Lefebvre. But none was forthcoming.

"Florida blue ink . . . ?"

For a few seconds, I thought he was onto something. But no—he simply didn't understand what "Florida blue" meant.

"A light aqua blue," I said.

"And did those letters come from France or abroad?"

He had asked as if he, too, were conducting an investigation.

"Unfortunately, I didn't notice the stamps."

"If I'd known, I would have warned Roger about her."

His voice had become metallic and his eyes very hard. Was this change of expression natural, or had he learned it at the Paupelix Course?

I'm trying to set down in black and white, as precisely as possible, the words we exchanged that day. But many of them have vanished. All those lost words, some of which you spoke yourself, others that you heard but have forgotten, and still others that were addressed to you but to which you paid no attention . . . And sometimes, on waking, or very late at night, the memory of a sentence returns from the past, but you don't know who whispered it.

He looked at his wristwatch and stood up sharply.

"I have to go to Rue Vaugelas . . . There might be some word of Roger and Noëlle . . ."

Was he hoping to find mail slid under the door, as I had at General Delivery shortly before?

"Can I come with you?"

"If you like . . . Roger gave me a key to the apartment."

"Did Noëlle come to this café often?" I asked.

And I was surprised at having called her by her given name, for the first time.

"Yes. Roger and I used to meet her here in the evenings, when she'd finished at Lancel. I was so happy when Roger got married . . . You know, there was no rivalry between Noëlle and me over Roger."

Apparently he hadn't been able to keep from blurting this out, but I sensed he immediately regretted it from the sudden flush of embarrassment on his face.

We followed Rue de la Convention due east, and I don't need to look at a map of Paris to realize today that it was away from the river, toward the bottom of Rue de Vaugirard.

"It's about a fifteen-minute walk," he said. "Is that okay for you?"

For the first time, he was showing a bit of fellow feeling. Was it relief at walking with someone, at that hour when night was falling and when the disappearances of Noëlle Lefebvre and Roger Behaviour must have weighed on him more than at any other time of day? And I told myself, too, that walking with him in this neighborhood might help me understand the life these three people led. The other evening, when handing me the fact sheet in its sky-blue folder, Hutte had given me an ironic smile. "Ball's in your court, kid. Figure it out! Nothing beats investigating in the field."

We walked past the post office where, earlier that afternoon, I had hoped they would hand me a letter for Noëlle Lefebvre. The post office was still open. I nearly suggested to Gérard Mourade that I go try at the window again: there might have been an evening delivery. But I checked myself in time. I preferred to go on my own, in the next few days. I saw no reason to involve this fellow too closely in my search. From now on, it was a private matter between Noëlle Lefebvre and me.

"So basically," I said to him, "the three of you lived a kind of neighborhood life around here?"

I was trying to find out what places, what people the three of them frequented.

"Not during the day. We only saw each other in the evening."

"And did you live around here too?"

"Yes, in a studio on Quai de Grenelle. Near a dance club we used to go to because Noëlle was fond of the place."

"A dance club?"

"The La Marine Dance Club, on the quay. But Roger and I never danced."

I was surprised by the remark, which he had spoken in very serious tones.

"You never danced?"

I think I'd put it ironically. But apparently he

wasn't in a joking mood. I concluded that the La Marine Dance Club was not to his taste.

"Roger knew the manager . . . Noëlle never mentioned it?"

He had asked the question as if it were a delicate subject.

"No, never. As I said, Noëlle didn't talk about her personal life, only about casual things . . . About Annecy, for instance, which we both knew."

He seemed relieved. Perhaps he had alluded to that dance hall and its "manager" to test the waters and find out whether Noëlle Lefebvre had vouchsafed something compromising.

"Roger met the manager when he worked for that moving company . . . that's all . . ."

I sensed there was no point in asking for more information—he wouldn't answer.

We walked the rest of the way side by side, in silence. To memorize the few names he'd given me concerning Noëlle Lefebvre, which weren't mentioned on the sheet, I repeated them to myself: Roger Behaviour, Lancel, La Marine Dance Club . . . It wasn't enough. I'd still need details that at first glance would seem unrelated, until the moment when enough pieces of the puzzle had been fitted together. And the only thing left would be to arrange them in order so that the whole picture might emerge, more or less.

"We can cut through here," he said.

We had come to the middle of Rue Olivier-de-Serres, and he pointed to a blind alley slicing between the buildings. It seems to me, with the passage of time, that it was lined with trees and that grass had sprouted between the cobblestones. The image I have today is of a country lane, perhaps because it was after dark. We crossed through a courtyard and emerged through a carriage door onto Rue Vaugelas.

Three small rooms on the ground floor. The window of one of them looked out on the street. The curtains weren't drawn, such that anyone passing by could have seen Gérard Mourade and me. Sometimes, in my dreams, I'm that passerby. Last night, no doubt because I'd written the preceding pages during the day, I again followed that country lane through the buildings. The apartment window was lit. With my forehead pressed against the glass, I could see where the light was coming from: the half-open door of the adjacent bedroom. A bedside lamp that someone had forgotten to turn off? Just as I was about to rap at the window, I woke up.

We were in the small room whose window looked out on the courtyard. Gérard Mourade had lit the lamp on a side table. This must have been the living room. A sofa and two leather armchairs.

"There are still some of Noëlle's clothes in the closet," Mourade said. "Roger took all his things with him, as if he didn't intend to come back."

This detail seemed to weigh on him. He stood beside me and kept silent.

"It's kind of strange that neither one has been in touch with you," I said.

He stood there, motionless, lost in thought.

"Would you wait here a minute?" he said. "I'm going to see the downstairs neighbor. He and Roger were friendly. Maybe he's heard something."

But I had the impression he didn't really believe it and that he'd said it just to comfort himself.

I found myself alone in the small living room whose window looked out on the courtyard. I switched off the lamp and, through the half-open door, slipped into the room facing the street. A fairly wide bed and a low bookcase running the length of the wall. I didn't turn on the bedside lamp for fear a passerby might spot me.

The faint light filtering in from outside was enough. I sat on the edge of the bed, near the nightstand, as if I'd been drawn there by a magnet and was rediscovering habits from a former life.

I pulled out the drawer of the nightstand. It was half the length of the table, which left room for a secret compartment. I reached in my arm and discovered a cardboard-covered notebook that someone had hidden there. I slid the drawer back in and, as I clutched the notebook in my hand, I heard Gérard Mourade slam the front door.

"Are you there? Are you in Noëlle and Roger's room?"

I didn't answer. I slipped the notebook into my inside jacket pocket and went to join him.

"Why did you turn off the light?"

"I was afraid someone would take me for a burglar if they saw a light in the window . . ."

I could have shown him the notebook, but I told myself he wouldn't understand why I'd taken it. And anyway, how could I explain? I'd done it as if in my sleep, in a trancelike state, and yet it was a precise, spontaneous action, as if I'd known in advance that in the nightstand, behind that drawer, there was a secret compartment where someone had stashed something. Hutte had said that one of the requisite qualities for this job was intuition. And in order to understand my action that evening, I'm consulting a dictionary as I write this. "Intuition: a form of

immediate knowledge, not dependent on con-
scious reasoning."

"Did you find out anything?" I asked.

"Nothing."

I hoped that in the notebook I'd just discovered, a door would open onto Noëlle Lefebvre.

"You should ask for information from other
people who knew them."

He shrugged. He didn't even think to switch
the lamp back on, and the two of us stood in the
twilight, in the middle of the small living room.

"Did she and her husband get along?"

"Oh, yes, very well. Otherwise I wouldn't
have advised Roger to marry her."

He had again taken on that superior tone.

"And neither you nor Roger Behaviour ever
thought of notifying the police about her disappearance?"

"The police? Why?"

No doubt about it, there wasn't much more
to be gotten from him. I was climbing a slippery
incline without any footholds. For a moment, I
was tempted to pull the notebook from my inner

pocket and suggest we discover together what Noëlle Lefebvre had written—for I was certain it was hers.

"And what about you? Since you knew her, maybe she'll get in touch with you?"

He suddenly seemed bereft and stared at me with uncertain eyes. Was there something else he wanted to tell me?

So he believed everything I'd said about Noëlle Lefebvre. And, in those days, I had such ease inserting myself into other people's lives that I wondered whether I actually did use to meet her in that café on Boulevard des Capucines, evenings after work.

"If she gets in touch," I told him, "I'll be sure to let you know."

We stayed there for a few more moments, the two of us standing in the twilight. Perhaps he was having the same feeling as I was: of having broken into an empty and long-abandoned apartment, whose last tenants had left no trace of their passage.

A black cloth-covered datebook with the year stamped in gold.

That same evening, I copied over on a blank sheet of paper the few things Noëlle Lefebvre had recorded. The datebook must have belonged to her, as her name was written at the top of the endpaper, in the same large handwriting and blue ink as the rest.

The last note was dated July 5th: *Gare de Lyon, 9:50*. From January to June, a few names, a few addresses, a few places and hours of appointments:

January 7	*Hôtel Bradford, 7 pm*
January 16	*Cook de Witting*
February 12	*Andrée Roger and Little Pierre, Rue Vitruve*
February 14	*Miki Durac, Boulevard Brune*
February 17	*The Magic Box, 13 Rue de la Félicité, 17th, 8 pm*
March 21	*Jeanne Faber*
April 17	*Josée, 5 Rue Yvon-Villarceau, 4 pm*
May 15	*Pierre Mollichi, Georges, La Marine Dance Club, 7 pm*

June 7   *Anita PRO-7674*
June 8   *Phone Mr. Bruneau*

On the page for June 10, she had jotted down a poem:

> *The sky is, above the roof,*
> *So calm, so fair!*
> *A branch, above the roof,*
> *Fans the air*

Monetary amounts, not in figures but spelled out:

January 3   *Six hundred francs*
February 14   *One thousand seven hundred francs*

On the page for February 11:

> *Train arr. Vierzon 5:37, Pruniers-en-Sologne–Chateau Chêne-Moreau*

On the page for April 16, an annotation, the longest in the datebook:

> *Per Georges, ask Marion Le Phat Vinh if she can get Roger a job in her transport company (Viot and Co., 5 Rue Cognacq-Jay)*

And this phrase, on June 28, in handwriting much larger than usual:

If I had known . . .

This supplemented Hutte's fact sheet, along with the names I had written down as soon as I returned from the 15th arrondissement:

Roger Behaviour
Gérard Mourade
Paupelix Course
Lancel
13 Rue Vaugelas
La Marine Dance Club

Not a lot. In the days following, I visited the addresses she'd jotted in her datebook—without jotting the house numbers, unfortunately. And on the afternoon when I found myself on Boulevard Brune between two rows of massive apartment buildings that seemed to stretch to infinity, I understood that I had no chance of finding Miki Durac on this boulevard, any more than Andrée Roger and Little Pierre on Rue Vitruve.

PRO-7674 didn't answer. No Anita. Impossible
to verify the names without addresses. I admit I
didn't feel up to going to Rue Yvon-Villarceau.
I contented myself with looking in the directory
and dialing the various phone numbers for the
building at number 5. And saying, each time,
"May I speak with Josée?" But after three nega-
tive replies, I got tired of repeating myself. In
short, the datebook gave the same nebulous impression as Hutte's fact sheet, which contained
so little detail. The approximate date and place
of birth of Noëlle Lefebvre; her supposed domi-
cile, 88 Rue de la Convention in the 15th arrondissement; a certain Brainos, who had given
Hutte the card she used for claiming her mail
at General Delivery. And this Brainos, with no
further indication, called himself "a friend of
Noëlle Lefebvre's."

Yes, indeed, there were quite a few blanks in
this life. The idea occurred to me as I flipped
through the many untouched pages of the datebook, even more strongly than when I'd read

the incomplete fact sheet in its sky-blue folder. Out of three hundred sixty-five days, only about twenty had caught Noëlle Lefebvre's notice, and with brief annotations, in her large handwriting, she had pulled them from the void. We'll never know how she spent her time, whom she met, or where she went on the other days. And amid all those blank, empty pages, I couldn't tear my eyes away from the phrase that surprised me every time I came across it: "If I had known . . ." It was like a voice breaking the silence, someone who started to confide in you but had a change of heart, or not enough time.

The investigation was going nowhere. One afternoon, I was again walking down Rue de la Convention to the post office, hoping to avoid Mourade. I waited at the General Delivery window. The man plucked an envelope from the pigeonhole after double-checking Noëlle Lefebvre's card. He returned and made me sign a register. He asked for identification. I presented my

Belgian passport. He seemed startled, slowly leafed through the pages, then shut the passport, glowering at its pale green cover as if he suspected the document was phony. I thought he'd never give me the letter. But then he brusquely handed over my Belgian passport, Noëlle Lefebvre's card, and the envelope.

Outside, I followed Rue de la Convention in the opposite direction. I slid the letter into one of my jacket pockets and walked quickly, like someone who feels he's being stalked. Again I was afraid of running into Mourade. Only after I'd put the Left Bank behind me and was on the Pont Mirabeau did I open the envelope.

Noëlle,

After our last phone conversation, I couldn't tell whether you wanted to see Sancho again and go back to Rome with him. That would be the best solution for you.

Sancho believed the two of you had reconciled when you got together last month at Caravelle and he was disappointed not to hear from you.

I went by the apartment on Rue de la Convention, but I found it empty and it looks like you've moved out. You for-

got your General Delivery card. Since I don't know where
to reach you at present, I hope you're still going there to get
your mail—with an identity card? Just in case, I'm sending
you this letter c/o General Delivery, and anyway I wonder
why you were so set on having people send your mail there
and what kind of mail it might be. Remember, I never gave
your address to Sancho, as promised, or told him you were
working at Lancel. But it has always been my intent to
bring the two of you back together and it seems to me the
time for that has come. The situation can't go on—I'm telling you this for your own good.

It would be best if you came to Chêne-Moreau and
stayed awhile. Sancho could join you there and you could
return to Rome together.

If you get this letter, tell me what you think of all this
and decide quickly. Paul Morihien could pick you up at
Vierzon station.

Call me as soon as you can.

GEORGES

PS: If you want to leave a message or get in touch with me,
you can always go see Pierre Mollichi at his office at La
Marine Dance Club, as you've done in the past.

The envelope was postmarked Paris—Rue
d'Anjou.

* * *

That evening, I showed the letter to Hutte and pointed out that the names "Vierzon" and "Chêne-Moreau" were also mentioned in Noëlle Lefebvre's datebook.

"So you think you're on to something?"

His tone was so blasé that it immediately deflated my fine confidence. As if undertaking a chore, he picked up the telephone receiver.

"I'd like the number for Chateau Chêne-Moreau in Pruniers-en-Sologne, please."

There was a long pause, during which I was afraid he'd simply hang up.

"I see . . . very well . . ."

He folded his arms and looked at me with a condescending smile.

"There's no listing for a Chateau Chêne-Moreau."

He noted my disappointment and added:

"Maybe we'd just need to know the name of the owner."

But he didn't seem terribly convinced this would work.

"Do you know anything about this Brainos who came to see you?" I asked.

"Yes, of course . . . I forgot to mention . . . To be honest, I don't feel overly enthusiastic about this case . . ."

With his index finger, he flicked through the block calendar on his desk.

"Brainos, Brainos . . . He came in last week, right?"

When he found the day, he leaned forward to read what he'd jotted down:

"Georges Brainos, 194 Avenue Victor-Hugo. He lives in Paris, but apparently used to manage some movie theaters in Brussels."

He let out a sigh, as if he'd just made a huge effort.

"A fairly sketchy character. In his fifties. He seemed very perturbed by this Noëlle Lefebvre's disappearance."

He opened the sky-blue folder that held the fact sheet, the card with Noëlle Lefebvre's photo, and the notes I'd taken following my investigation in the field, as he called it. And the letter from General Delivery, signed Georges. Georges Brainos.

"Thank you for the additional information. Brainos hadn't told me she was married, or that she worked at Lancel."

He gave me a slightly embarrassed smile, seeming to choose his words carefully so as not to hurt my feelings.

"You see, my boy, I just don't think this case is worth it. It will be a lot of work for nothing. As clients go, that man doesn't strike me as especially reliable. Are you disappointed? You deserve better. Soon I'll put you on a more consequential matter."

But no, I wasn't at all looking at it from a professional viewpoint. The disappearance of Noëlle Lefebvre had awakened much deeper echoes in me, so deep that I would have had trouble elucidating them.

"You're mistaken," I said. "I'm not disappointed at all."

I was even relieved at the thought that he took no interest in the case. From this point on, it concerned only me. I was no longer accountable to him. He was giving me free rein.

Yes, that's what I thought at the time. But today, as I write this and again see myself standing before Hutte, he leaning with folded arms against the edge of his desk, his ultramarine eyes fixed on me with paternal attention, I feel a need to rectify the preceding lines. It was he who deliberately led me to my search. Without saying a word, he knew everything, from the outset, but he preferred to give me an incomplete file. He had perhaps guessed how deeply I was implicated in this "case," and in a few words he could have revealed the smallest details and enlightened me about myself. "Soon I'll put you on a more consequential matter." I was too young at the time to understand what that sentence meant. It was a discreet and affectionate way of standing back and letting me find the path on my own. He wished me well. He'd given me a few clues. It was my job to follow up. I had reached the age where one has to assume one's responsibilities. If he gave me free rein, it's because he'd guessed that I would write all this later.

There are blanks in a life, but also sometimes what they call a refrain. For periods of varying length, you don't hear this refrain, as if you've forgotten it. And then one day, it comes back to you unbidden, when you're alone and there are no distractions. It comes back, like the words of a children's song that still has a hold on you.

I'm counting the years and trying to be as precise as possible: cross-checking dates, I'd say that ten years had passed since my brief apprenticeship at the Hutte Agency and those afternoons when I'd gone to General Delivery in search of Noëlle Lefebvre. To no avail. Except for the meager file in the sky-blue folder, which I'd kept and which wasn't even as thick as police files of dismissed cases.

I happened to be in a small barbershop on Rue des Mathurins, awaiting my turn near a coffee table that held several stacks of magazines and a cinema yearbook. The volume's brown cover displayed its year of publication: 1970.

I leafed through it and came to the part featuring "photos of the artists." A name jumped out at me: Gérard Mourade. Still, it's true I hadn't thought of that name in ten years. While "Noëlle Lefebvre" remained clearly etched in my memory, I would have had trouble recalling, if asked point blank, the exact name of the man I had met a decade earlier, one April in a café.

In the photo, he was wearing the same sheepskin jacket as when he'd first talked with me. A leather cap pushed back off his forehead and a scarf, tightly knotted around his neck . . . He was perched on the arm of a chair and smiling. Below the photo was a telephone number written in red pencil.

The barber had noticed me looking through the yearbook, and when I was seated in the swivel chair in front of the mirror and draped in a white smock, he said:

"Are you a film buff, sir?"

"I found a friend's picture in that yearbook."

It surprised me to admit that. I had nearly

forgotten Mourade, and here he was, suddenly reappearing.

"I might have met him. I spent quite a few years doing makeup for the movies."

Was he the one who'd written the phone number in red pencil? He picked up the yearbook from the coffee table and I pointed out Mourade's photo, which he contemplated.

He didn't seem to know him.

"And yet, that's my handwriting, here, in red pencil . . . He came in for a haircut . . ."

He stretched his arm toward the other side of the street, past his shop window.

"He must have had a bit part in one of those theaters across the way. But when? They come and they go . . . So many . . . It's hard to remember them all . . . Are you an actor, too, sir?"

"Not exactly."

"If you knew how many I've done makeup for—actors, that is . . ."

A sorrowful expression clouded his eyes. He held the cinema yearbook in his hand.

"You can have this. Maybe you'll find some more friends in it."

In the street, I felt like ridding myself of that yearbook, which weighed a ton. But no, I'd put it in a drawer. The photo of Gérard Mourade would be one more clue, after the fact sheet drawn up by Hutte ten years earlier, the paltry two pages of information I'd added to it, and the letter to Noëlle Lefebvre I'd retrieved at General Delivery. One more clue? I thought of court trials in which they present the so-called "evidence," and in particular of one trial from after the war: behind the accused were about thirty suitcases—the only remaining traces of persons who had gone missing.

Before stashing it in the drawer, I opened the yearbook and looked again at the photo of Gérard Mourade. His black leather cap pushed back off his forehead, his smile and rakish pose hardly corresponded to the young man with whom I'd spent an afternoon in the 15th arrondissement. That day, he had seemed much gloomier. The successive disappearances of Noëlle Lefebvre and Roger Behaviour were only several weeks old at the time, which explained his edginess and anxiety. But here, on the photo, five years later, he had no doubt resigned himself to their absence. Or perhaps, quite simply, he'd heard from them and they had all been reunited.

Printed under the photo was not his address, but that of a talent agent.

I decided to phone. A woman answered, probably the secretary.

"I'm trying to get in touch with one of your artists," I said.

"The artist's name, sir?"

"Gérard Mourade."

"And how do you spell that?"

I spelled out the name.

A pause. Then paper rustling. She must have been consulting a file.

"Mourade, Gérard . . . Our office stopped handling his account in 1971, sir."

"Do you have his address?"

"We have two addresses, one at 57 Quai de

Grenelle in Paris, and the other in Maisons-
Alfort, 26 Rue Carnot. We got him a small part
in a play in 1969, *The End of the World,* at the
Théâtre Michel. That's all I can tell you, sir."

What was the point of going to Quai de Grenelle, in the same neighborhood where I had
followed in Noëlle Lefebvre's footsteps? I didn't
have the courage. Or the time. And besides, it
would have felt like going backward, to a period
when my life was still deeply unresolved. But
that was no longer the case, and I really didn't
see what role a Gérard Mourade could now play
in it.

Toward evening, I had a change of heart. I
didn't want to have any regrets, or rather, any
remorse. I took a metro line I hadn't ridden
in ten years. At Javel station, I walked up the
quay toward the Pont de Grenelle. Still, once I
reached the bridge, I wondered if it was really
worth going any farther. They had knocked
down the buildings facing the river and, in their
place, all that remained were empty lots and
heaps of rubble. It was as if there had been a

bombardment on this no-man's-land that they would later baptize the Front de Seine. And it hadn't spared the first building on the quay after the bridge, of which all that remained was the concrete façade. I might have mistaken it for the façade of a former garage if I hadn't read, above the gaping doorway, the sign in red lettering: La Marine Dance Club.

Another afternoon in Paris, in July, in the sweltering heat. I had gone looking for fresher air in the Bois de Boulogne, and I was waiting for the 63 bus to take me back to the center of town. But I changed my mind and instead walked to the start of Avenue Victor-Hugo.

A name had popped into my memory, that of Georges Brainos, whom Hutte had met in his office long ago and who had reported the disappearance of Noëlle Lefebvre; the Brainos whose letter I had retrieved at the General Delivery window. I remembered his address, 194 Avenue Victor-Hugo, from having reread so often the few incomplete notes in the file.

I've just written the phrase "long ago" in the preceding paragraph. It applies equally well to that July afternoon, which now seems so far away that I can't say precisely which year it was: before or after my visit to the barber's where I came across the photo of Mourade, or perhaps the same year as when I ran into Jacques B., aka "the Marquis"?

I followed the avenue on the left, the even-numbered side, and soon arrived at number 194, a small town house with a brick-and-stone façade, on which the metal shutters were closed over every window. A copper plaque attached to the front door seemed fairly new, even though the building itself looked abandoned. On the plaque, I read in black letters: "La Caravelle Real Estate, P. Mollichi." And that name, like "194 Avenue Victor-Hugo," also figured in my old notes.

I hesitated a few minutes, then pressed the doorbell, certain no one would answer. The heat, the deserted neighborhood in July, the façade with its closed shutters . . . But I was surprised by the strident timbre of the bell, which sliced through the afternoon torpor. It would have awoken you from the deepest slumber.

The door opened immediately, as if someone had been standing right behind it, waiting for a visitor. A man looked me over: short, with receding hairline, dry features as if they'd been whittled in pale wood, and faintly slanting eyes. He was wearing a tight-fitting dark suit.

"I'd like to speak with Mr. Mollichi, please."

I tried to make my voice sound firm.

"I'm he."

He gave me a smile as dry as his face and did not seem at all surprised by my visit. He bade me enter and closed the door behind him.

He ushered me into a room on the ground floor and motioned toward a seat facing a trestle table that must have served as his desk, judging from the many folders stacked up on it.

"What can I do for you?"

He had put a certain friendliness, I would even say a certain joviality, into the question. And it clashed with his inexpressive facial features.

"I was simply hoping for some information."

The heat was even more oppressive in this room than outside, and I mopped my brow with my shirtsleeve. But it didn't seem to bother him, despite his very high, tight collar, tie, and cinched jacket. As the shutters were closed, the glare from the chandelier was blinding.

"It's about a friend I haven't heard from in quite some time, who knew Mr. Brainos."

Sitting at his desk, bolt upright, he looked at me with what appeared to be benevolence. Perhaps my visit took his mind off the monotony of his workday. He noticed I was sweating.

"I'm so sorry . . . I wish I could offer you something cool to drink . . ."

He paused a moment before adding:

"I was in fact Mr. Brainos's secretary, then his business partner. And now I manage his affairs. Mr. Brainos passed away last year in Lausanne."

There was a moment of silence. A thought crossed my mind: one more witness who has taken his secrets with him.

"And you remembered that Mr. Brainos had lived here, I suppose?"

"Yes."

"Unfortunately we'll be obliged to tear this

building down in a few months. For some new construction."

He seemed truly sorry. He had a pencil in his hand, with which he tapped on the edge of the table.

"And what was your friend's name?"

"Noëlle . . . Noëlle Lefebvre . . ."

He was gazing at me, but I sensed he wasn't really seeing me. Apparently he was making an effort to remember something.

"I must have met her . . . That goes back about ten years . . . Noëlle . . . Right . . . Mr. Brainos was very fond of her . . ."

He smiled at me. He was relieved to be able to place this Noëlle.

"She came to see me several times at the La Marine Dance Club . . ."

He leaned toward me with the hint of a smile.

"The name might surprise you . . . I'll explain briefly . . . Mr. Brainos's organization initially controlled movie theaters in Brussels, as well as a company dealing in spare auto parts . . ."

He had adopted a businesslike tone, as if delivering a report.

"After that, Mr. Brainos created a company that operated the La Marine Dance Club on Quai de Grenelle and La Caravelle, a restaurant near the Champs-Elysées . . . Mr. Brainos had appointed me manager of the dance club, a business from which he then divested himself . . ."

His pencil was now tapping the palm of his hand.

"I'm telling you this because the young woman in question came to the dance club several times to bring me letters for Mr. Brainos. And on a few occasions, I had a letter from Mr. Brainos to give to her."

He seemed glad to have someone with whom he could talk about "Mr. Brainos." Here, in the month of July, in his office with the closed shutters, the afternoons must have dragged on interminably.

"Sometimes she came to La Marine in the evening with friends . . . But I didn't think it was a suitable place for her . . ."

He fell silent and I wondered whether he had forgotten my presence, but clearly he was searching for other memories.

"She even lived here for a while . . . in one of the upstairs rooms . . . That's all I can tell you about her . . ."

He seemed to be apologizing for not knowing more about Noëlle Lefebvre.

"Mr. Brainos would surely have been able to provide further details."

"He died in Lausanne?"

I don't know why I'd blurted out that question.

"Sadly, one can die anywhere. Even in Lausanne . . ."

He gave me a sorrowful stare.

"You wouldn't possibly have known a friend of Mr. Brainos, a certain Sancho, would you?" I asked.

"No. No, that name doesn't ring a bell. You know, as the manager and sales director, I only knew the people who did business with Mr. Brainos, or rather his close associates . . ."

He again assumed a professional tone.

"At the Caravelle company, he worked with Mr. Anselme Escautier, Othon de Bogaerde, Mme. Marion Le Phat Vinh, Mr. Serge Servoz . . ."

Those two final names stirred something in me, without my being able to say exactly what at the time.

"Yes, I understand," I said to interrupt him, as I feared the list might drag on. "So, you knew that the young woman had temporarily lived here in one of the upstairs rooms?"

"Yes. When she first came to Paris. I think Mr. Brainos had known her in the provinces. He had given her an affectionate nickname, 'the Shepherdess of the Alps.' But I don't know any more than that. Were the two of you close?"

"Very close."

"And you don't know what became of her?"

"No."

"And was it from her that you heard of Mr. Brainos?"

"Yes. I was hoping he could tell me where she is."

"I understand."

A long silence passed between us.

"I'm in the midst of organizing Mr. Brainos's rather complicated business dealings. Including his papers. If I come across anything regarding this Noëlle . . . Noëlle—what was it?"

"Lefebvre."

He jotted the name on a sheet of paper.

"I will gladly let you know. Tell me how to reach you."

I gave him my name and phone number. He handed me his business card.

"Come back anytime. I'm in the office all day. Even in July."

As I was leaving, I gazed at the lit chandelier above us, a chandelier of impressive size. He saw me looking.

"This used to be the salon. In the time of Mr. Brainos."

Outside, the air was less stifling than before. I couldn't help thinking about that man, in his office behind closed shutters, beneath the blinding light of the chandelier, bolt upright, tie knotted, without a single drop of perspiration on his brow. I wondered if I hadn't dreamed it all, if I should go back to verify whether the façade of number 194 was still there, or whether the town house had already been demolished "for some new construction," as Pierre Mollichi had specified.

I'd forgotten to ask him about the Chateau Chêne-Moreau in Pruniers-en-Sologne, the name of which figured in both Georges Brainos's letter and Noëlle Lefebvre's datebook. But what was the point? I was certain his answer would have been vague, as vague as the few details he'd provided concerning Noëlle Lefebvre.

I could count only on myself, and that, instead of discouraging me, caused me a certain euphoria. I walked along the avenue toward Place de l'Etoile and felt, that evening, in what is oddly called an "altered state." Never had Paris seemed so gentle and kind, never had I gone so far into the heart of summer, the season that a philosopher whose name I've forgotten qualified as metaphysical. And so Noëlle, the Shepherdess of the Alps, had lived for a time in one of the upstairs rooms, just a few hundred yards behind me . . . The avenue was deserted, and yet I felt a presence by my side; the air was keener than what I normally breathed, the evening and the summer more phosphorescent. And this I felt each time I ventured onto side streets so that I might then record my itinerary in black and white, each time I lived a different life—on the fringes of my life.

Today I begin the sixty-ninth page of this book, thinking that the Internet is no help to me at all. No trace on it of Gérard Mourade, or of Roger Behaviour. The search engine turns up three Noëlle Lefebvres in France, but none corresponds to the woman who received mail at General Delivery.

So much the better, for there would be nothing left to write a book about. You'd only have to copy down sentences that appear on your screen, without the slightest effort of imagination.

And, as with digital photos, you would no longer see the image slowly develop in a darkroom, the image and darkroom mentioned by a writer from the nineteenth century, in a letter I might have found at General Delivery after it had been forgotten there for more than a hundred years, and which would have given me the courage to go on: "I still talk to no one. Moreover, it is in this kind of darkroom of solitude that I must see my books come to life before I can write them."

Perhaps it would be simpler to follow chronological order, based on a horde of reference
points. My datebooks are even emptier than the
one belonging to Noëlle Lefebvre, which I'd
found in the secret compartment of the nightstand. And anyway, truth be told, I've never
owned a datebook and never kept a diary. It
would have made my job easier. But I didn't
want to quantify my life. I let it flow by, like mad
money that slips through your fingers. I wasn't
careful. When I thought about the future, I told
myself that none of what I had lived through
would ever be lost. None of it. I was too young
to know that after a certain point, you start trip-
ping over gaps in your memory.

Having recalled my visit to that barber on
Rue des Mathurins and Mourade's photo in the
cinema yearbook, I notice that I've indeed had
what they call a memory lapse. I wrote earlier
that ten years had passed since the spring afternoon when Hutte sent me "into the field" to look
for Noëlle Lefebvre. And thus I left the impression that, during those ten years, I'd given no

further thought to that brief episode in my life, and that all the people I'd met and the events I'd experienced in those ten years had covered that afternoon with a blanket of amnesia. But no. From now on, I must force myself to respect chronological order as much as possible, or else I'll get lost in those spaces where memory blurs into forgetting.

It can't have been more than two years after I left the Hutte Agency. Suddenly, one afternoon, on the sidewalk, I received a shock, as if time were yanking me backward, or rather as if those two years had been obliterated. And once again I felt like I was back on the trail.

I was crossing the plaza in front of the Opéra and was about to go down the steps of the metro, when from a distance I saw the sign and display window of the Lancel leather goods shop. The sidewalk buckled for a fraction of a second, making me stumble and rousing me from a long sleep.

Without a moment's hesitation, I walked into Lancel and up to one of the saleswomen at the back of the shop.

"Pardon me. I'm looking for information about Noëlle Lefebvre."

I had said it in a firm voice, clearly articulating each syllable, but she didn't seem to understand.

"Information about who, sir?"

She looked at me warily and I was afraid she would alert her colleagues. I certainly didn't look like their standard clientele.

"Noëlle Lefebvre. She worked here two years ago."

"I've only been here six months . . . You'll have to ask my colleague . . ."

She pointed to a brunette of about thirty, sitting at a desk not far from the shop entrance.

She hadn't noticed my presence. She was absorbed in what seemed to be accounts. I was about to leave as quietly as I could when she looked up at me.

"Madam . . . Could you possibly give me any information about Noëlle Lefebvre . . . ? She used to work here about two years ago . . ."

She didn't take her eyes off me, as if trying to gauge what sort of person she might be dealing with. My outfit was sober and my hair of classic cut. I had asked the question in a very calm voice. I had nothing to regret.

"Were you a friend of Noëlle Lefebvre's?"

I sensed that I'd piqued her interest. The only worrisome thing was that she had used the past tense.

"Yes. A very good friend."

"We close in an hour . . . It's hard to talk here . . . We can meet across the street if you like, on Boulevard des Capucines, at the Café Khédive . . . In an hour . . ."

She stood up, walked me to the exit, and pointed out the café.

I took a seat at a table on the terrace. Two years earlier, when I was trying to find out more, I had told Gérard Mourade that this was the café where I met up with Noëlle Lefebvre after work. And as more time passed, I began to wonder whether what I'd said to Mourade really was a lie. I was sorry not to have the General Delivery card on me so I could study the photo more closely. Might I actually have met Noëlle Lefebvre? There are blanks in a life, and ellipses in memory. And if I had taken seriously the investigation Hutte had assigned to me—a fairly mundane "case," since hundreds of people disappear every day, or change address, or simply break with their routine on a whim—it was no doubt because that face reminded me of something, someone I might have known by another name.

I saw her crossing the street and waved. She stood by my table.

"Would you mind walking me to La Madeleine? That's where I take the metro . . . I have to be home a bit early . . ."

We passed by the Lancel shop window and crossed the plaza. She remained silent. We wouldn't have much time before reaching La Madeleine. It was up to me to break the ice.

"You were a friend of Noëlle Lefebvre's?"

"Yes. As soon as she started at Lancel. We often went out together."

She seemed relieved that I had taken the first step, as if it were about a delicate subject.

"And you haven't heard from her?"

"No. Not for the past two years."

"Neither have I."

It was rush hour on the sidewalk of Boulevard

des Capucines. People poured out of their offices and went to take the metro or the train at Saint-Lazare. I had the impression that all of them were heading against us and I was afraid we'd lose each other in the crowd, especially since she was walking fast and I was having trouble keeping up with her. It would have been easier and safer to hold her arm, but she might have taken it amiss.

"And you have no idea where she might be these days?"

"None. Her husband came to Lancel. I talked to him. He couldn't understand it, either."

I sensed it was painful for her to evoke those memories. And, after all these years, I wonder whether she'd preferred that we talk about Noëlle Lefebvre in a crowd, rather than face to face in a café.

"Did you know her husband well?"

"Not really. I must have seen him a few times. We always went out just the two of us, Noëlle and I."

"And did you meet Gérard Mourade?"

"The tall dark-haired guy who took acting lessons?"

She had raised her face toward me. She had an ironic smile.

"Noëlle brought me to his drama class once . . . it was right near Lancel . . ."

She was walking so fast that I had trouble not only keeping up, but hearing what she said. Aside from which, her muffled voice didn't carry.

"And what about you, did you know her husband?" she asked.

"No."

"She told me he was kind of a depressive sort. She was always trying to find him work. Anyway, I wonder if he really was her husband . . ."

A note in Noëlle Lefebvre's datebook came back to mind, among all the ones I knew by heart from trying so hard to decipher them, as if they were in secret code: "Ask Marion Le Phat Vinh if she can get Roger a job in her transport company."

"You think he wasn't her husband?"

"I think Noëlle had a rather complicated love life and it sometimes made things difficult for her . . . But she never confided in me about it . . ."

"So, the two of you used to go out together?"

If I didn't ask questions, I felt she would have kept silent. Noëlle Lefebvre's disappearance was surely a painful subject for her. Over the span of two years, she must have thought about it, like me, in increasingly distant intervals, since daily life eventually has to reassert itself.

"Yes, we went out together. Sometimes she took me to some very odd places. Like a dancing club on Quai de Grenelle."

"La Marine?"

"Yes, La Marine. Did she take you there too?"

She stopped walking, as if she were expecting a reply and it mattered to her.

"No. Never."

"It's funny," she said. "I feel like I once saw you with her in that café from before . . . the one opposite Lancel . . ."

"No. You're mistaken."

"Then it must have been someone who looked like you . . ."

We stood apart from the crowd, at the top of the alley that led to the Edouard VII theater. It was empty, and this contrasted with the flood of pedestrians on the boulevard, where we'd had to walk against the current.

"And there was another place Noëlle often took me, not La Marine . . . near the Champs-Elysées . . . at the start of an alley . . . like the one we're in now . . ."

She glanced at her wristwatch.

"I'm running late . . . forgive me."

She had resumed walking, and I had as much trouble keeping up with her in that crowd as before. She kept silent and seemed preoccupied. It was as if she had forgotten my presence and all about Noëlle Lefebvre.

"So basically," I said to her, "you only knew her for a few months?"

"About three months. But we were really close."

She suddenly adopted a very serious tone. And I was surprised when she took my arm.

"And what about you—did you know her long?"

"Yes. Very long. We were born in the same region. Near Annecy."

It was the same thing I'd said to Mourade two years earlier. And that evening, repeating it, I felt as if it wasn't entirely false.

"I knew she was born in a village in the mountains, but she never mentioned you . . ."

"We didn't see much of each other in those last years . . . I think she'd made some new friends . . ."

I wanted to cite a name, but the name escaped me. And then, out of the blue, I remembered it.

"Do you know a friend of hers called Georges Brainos? A man in his fifties . . ."

She seemed to think about it, still holding onto my arm.

"In his fifties? That must have been the owner of the dance club and that other place I told you

about, near the Champs-Elysées . . . or perhaps
someone else . . ."

Brainos didn't seem to interest her much.
Again she fell silent, and I couldn't think of
any further questions to ask. We arrived at La
Madeleine. We were at the metro entrance.

"She had another friend besides me . . . Miki
Durac . . . I don't know where they met. She
introduced Noëlle to a lot of people . . . But I
preferred to see her alone . . . Have you met
Miki Durac?"

She looked at me distrustfully. She didn't
seem to like this Miki Durac very much.

"No, I never met her."

"We haven't had much time to talk about
Noëlle," she said. "We can meet again if you
like . . ."

She opened her handbag and handed me her
card. It was hard for us to stand there, at the
entrance to the metro, without getting jostled.
Rush hour.

We shook hands. I felt she wanted to tell me
something.

"Listen . . . I've been trying to come up with an explanation . . . I think she must be dead . . ."

And then she left me suddenly, as if carried away by the tide of all those people descending the stairs.

Not long afterward, I had a moment's fright that I'd lost her card. But it was in one of my trouser pockets. Françoise Steur. An address and phone number in Levallois-Perret. "I think she must be dead." She had said this in her muffled voice, and I'd had trouble hearing her.

Ponder it as I might, I couldn't reconcile myself to the idea. When I think back on it today, I tell myself that her decisive statement, "I think she must be dead," didn't correspond to the vagueness and uncertainty that surrounded Noëlle Lefebvre in my mind. If it had simply been a matter of gathering all the pieces of a puzzle and obtaining a precise and definitive image, perhaps the statement wouldn't have shocked me as it had when I stood that evening with Françoise Steur by the stairs to the metro.

But no matter how much you scrutinize the details of what has been a life, there will always remain secrets and receding lines. And to me, this seemed the opposite of death.

On top of which, another aspect of the question appears to me more clearly today than when I was young: can you trust witnesses? What had Gérard Mourade or Françoise Steur told me regarding Noëlle Lefebvre that had really enlightened me about her? Not much. A few disjointed, contradictory details that muddled everything, like radio static that keeps you from listening to a piece of music. And those witnesses are so implausible that you meet them once, ask questions to which they provide no answers, and don't feel any need to stay in touch.

This wasn't the case with Françoise Steur, whom I saw again later, and I'll say more about that if I feel up to it. But Gérard Mourade? When I left the barbershop on Rue des Mathurins, with that film yearbook in hand, I thought to myself that not once in the previous five years had I given him a thought. Still, had I been more curious, I could have learned that he played a bit part in *The End of the World* at the Théâtre Michel and gone to see him in his dressing room. But chances are I would have been disappointed: he might have forgotten all about Noëlle Lefebvre and our first encounter. As far as Miki Durac was concerned, I had given up two years earlier trying to find her among the countless buildings on Boulevard Brune.

I wish I could follow chronological order and set down the moments in those many years when Noëlle Lefebvre again crossed my mind, specifying the date and hour of each instance. But it's impossible to draw up that sort of calendar after such a long time. I think it's better to let the writing flow. Yes, memories occur as the pen flies. You shouldn't force them, but just write, crossing out as little as possible. And in the uninterrupted flood of words and sentences, a few details, which you've forgotten or buried at the bottom of your memory, who knows why, will slowly rise to the surface. Above all, don't break momentum, but rather keep in mind the image of a skier gliding for all eternity down a steep trail, like the pen on a blank page. There will be time enough later for cross-outs.

A skier gliding for all eternity. Today, those words evoke for me the Haute-Savoie, where I spent several years of my adolescence. Annecy, Veyrier-du-Lac, Megève, Mont d'Arbois . . .

One July afternoon at Richelieu-Drouot, in

the same year that I found Mourade's photo in the cinema yearbook, I ran into a friend from none other than Annecy, a certain Jacques B., whom we'd nicknamed "the Marquis." And just then, I remembered that Noëlle Lefebvre was born in "a village near Annecy." I hadn't ascribed too much importance to this detail on Hutte's fact sheet. That sheet was so fragmentary, riddled with so many inaccuracies, that I wondered whether Hutte himself hadn't made up the "village near Annecy" to give Noëlle Lefebvre a place of birth and have done with a "case" that didn't interest him.

I hadn't seen Jacques B. in ten years, as with everyone else I'd known in Haute-Savoie.

He told me he was working for a newspaper down the street, and we found ourselves sitting across a table in the Café Cardinal.

The room was empty. Because of the Marquis's presence, it felt as if we were back under the arcades of the Taverne, in Annecy, in the middle of a summer afternoon.

I let the Marquis tell me about his "journey,"

as he called it, since the good old days of Annecy. A stint in the Foreign Legion. Discharged after several months. Minor jobs in Lyon before catching a train to Paris. And he'd ended up becoming a journalist, covering human interest stories. For the past two years.

"Why the Foreign Legion?" I asked.

He had seemed so casual, so carefree back then, on the beach and in the streets of Annecy, that I would never have foreseen his enlistment.

"Just because," he said with a shrug. "I didn't have much choice . . ."

And I chided myself for not having sensed his malaise back then.

"In Annecy, did you ever know someone named Lefebvre?"

"With or without a *b?*"

I recognized his sarcastic smile, a smile that, in my memory, never left his lips.

"With a *b*."

"Le*feb*vre . . ."

He pronounced the name, stressing the letter *b*.

"But of course . . . Sancho Lefebvre."

Sancho Lefebvre. That name also rang a bell for me. But I never would have associated him with Noëlle Lefebvre.

"He was a bit older than us . . . You wouldn't have known him . . . I can't think of any other Lefebvres in Annecy . . . But what do you care about Sancho Lefebvre?"

He gazed at me with his eternal smile, not seeming surprised, just a bit taken aback that this Sancho Lefebvre should show up there, beside us, like a ghost, or perhaps a cadaver.

"He must have left Annecy a good fifteen years ago . . . But he'd come back now and again . . . He lived in Switzerland or Rome . . . or maybe Paris . . ."

And, all of a sudden, I remembered the beginning of a summer afternoon in Annecy. I had taken refuge in the lobby of a hotel on Rue Sommeiller to escape the sun and heat. Three or four people were sitting near me and the name "Sancho Lefebvre" kept cropping up in their conversation, without my being able to grasp what they were saying—other than that name, Sancho. The same name was mentioned in the letter to Noëlle Lefebvre that I had intercepted ten years earlier, at General Delivery.

"An odd duck . . . We always knew when he was back in Annecy because of his car . . . an English or Italian sports job . . . or an American convertible . . ."

"How old would he be now?"

"Oh, thirty-nine or forty."

"Was he married?"

"Nah."

Sitting opposite me, Jacques B. seemed lost in thought.

"That last year in Annecy, before I signed up for the Legion . . . I think you and I were still in touch back then, weren't we? In sixty-two or sixty-three . . . I heard that Sancho Lefebvre had left Annecy with a girl of twenty . . . and even that he'd married her . . ."

"Did you know the girl?"

"No."

"Her name wasn't Noëlle, by any chance?"

"I never knew a Noëlle in Annecy."

We had exhausted the subject. I'd had some qualms about asking him all those questions and I tried to find words to explain.

"It has to do with an incident a friend was mixed up in about ten years ago . . . someone's disappearance . . . and since the girl was born near Annecy, I thought you might know about it . . ."

"An incident? Why not? With a guy like Sancho Lefebvre, anything was possible."

He had used the past tense. And, all at once, I felt a great weariness at bringing up the past and its mysteries. It was a little like the people who had tried, over dozens and dozens of years, to decrypt an ancient language. Like Etruscan.

We talked about everyday matters in contemporary language. And then, after exchanging addresses and phone numbers, I walked him to Rue de Richelieu, to the offices of his newspaper. As he was heading into the lobby, he smiled and said:

"If you like, I can try to find out more about Sancho Lefebvre."

I remember my state of mind that day. After leaving Jacques B., aka "the Marquis," I had walked down the wide boulevards. Nearing the Rex cinema, I told myself I would go look up Françoise Steur, only a few yards away. But did she still work at Lancel? If so, she would make me wait an hour or two before she could leave the shop. What was the use? No doubt she was unaware of Sancho Lefebvre's existence.

I was stumped. It now seemed certain that Noëlle Lefebvre had never officially been called Noëlle Behaviour, but that she'd been married to this faceless man whom Jacques B. said I couldn't have known in Annecy. Mme. Sancho Lefebvre. And what was her maiden name? She had not merely vanished ten years earlier, for me she was now nameless. Even her first name, Noëlle — was it real?

Several times over the following days I felt the urge to telephone Jacques B. and propose another get-together. He was the only person I could talk to about that period of my life in Haute-Savoie. And the fact that the enigmatic Sancho Lefebvre and Noëlle Lefebvre were both connected to that region troubled me. A very common name in France, Lefebvre, and probably in Haute-Savoie as well.

I had to work it out on my own, without the assistance of Jacques B. I tried to make a list of everyone I'd known in Haute-Savoie, in hopes that one of them might suddenly lead me to Sancho or Noëlle Lefebvre. I have to admit it was rough going at first. I felt like an amnesiac who has been handed a very detailed route that he has to follow in a place that was once familiar. The name of a village alone might suddenly call up his entire past.

It was the first time I'd indulged in this sort of exercise. When Hutte had sent me to the 15th arrondissement to look for Noëlle Lefebvre and I knew, from the fact sheet he'd written, that she was born "in a village near Annecy," I hadn't made a direct connection with my own stay in Haute-Savoie. My memories of that stay were still fresh, since the last of them were barely three years old. But I was neither accustomed nor inclined to look to the past.

I was amazed that so many names came back to me. I jotted them in a notebook, and the faces corresponding to those names paraded by like a slide show. Some faces had relatively clear features, while others were so fuzzy that they were little more than a halo or vague outline, in which barely the mouth and eyebrows emerged. Though most of those faces were no longer recognizable, the names had remained intact.

Loulou Alauzet, Georges Panisset, Yerta Royez, Mme. Chevallier, Doctor Besson, Doctor Trevoux, Pimpin Lavorel, Zazie, Marie-France, Pierrette, Fanchon, Kurt Wick, Rosy, Chantal, Robert Constantin, Pierre Andrieux, and other names kept flooding in . . . But even though I kept murmuring them to myself, none was linked for me with Sancho Lefebvre, whose name I had heard mentioned one summer afternoon in the lobby of a hotel on Rue Sommeiller by people I didn't know. It even seemed I was heading down the wrong path. If I tried to recall all the people I'd known in Haute-Savoie at the time, Sancho Lefebvre and the eponymous Noëlle would be lost in the crowd, and I'd forfeit all chance of finding them. I had indeed chosen a very poor method. The brutal rush of memories risked obscuring other, more secret ones, and covering their tracks forever.

But thinking again about Jacques B. and our conversation, I found my way back to a path where I had some hope of meeting Sancho Lefebvre. Something Jacques B. had said, which hadn't struck me at first, sounded again in my mind, more clearly this time: "An odd duck . . . We always knew when he was back in Annecy because of his car . . ." And the image of an American convertible gradually imposed itself on me, as if I were waiting for a photo to develop in a darkroom. I had seen it several times during one of those torrid summers at the beginning of the 1960s, parked in different spots along Avenue d'Albigny, on the left-hand sidewalk in front of the police station, or on the right-hand one near the Sporting. And also in front of the casino's café. But which summer, exactly? One early afternoon, I was walking up the path from the beach at Veyrier-du-Lac to buy a newspaper in the little roadside shop, before the post office and the church. On the front page, huge black letters spelled out a name I didn't know, but that struck me because of its sonority: BIZERTE — a dull, disquieting sonority, like the two syllables I'd learned to read as a child, in the twilight of auto repair garages: CASTROL. I'd have only to look up the date of the so-called "Bizerte crisis" to reconstruct which year it was.

It must have been the first summer I spent in Annecy after a year of boarding school in a neighboring village. I was coming out of the casino cinema. It was around midnight. I could return to my room in Veyrier-du-Lac on foot, but it would take a while. Or I could hitchhike. Or wait until six o'clock and take the first bus out of Place de la Gare. It was then that I saw a boy coming toward me whom I'd met the week before on the beach at Marquisats, an older boy named Daniel V. Since the start of the holidays, V. had been earning pocket money by giving tennis lessons, but he'd told me he intended to leave Annecy for good in October to "work in the hotel industry in Geneva or Paris." He already had a little experience in the trade from tending bar for six months at the Cintra on Rue Vaugelas.

"What brings you here all on your own?"

I told him I had to get back to Veyrier-du-Lac but wasn't sure how. Probably on foot.

"No, come on . . . I'll take you there . . ."

And he flashed me a wide grin, like a bartender suggesting one more cocktail to a lone customer who has lingered late.

He pulled me toward Avenue d'Albigny.

"I've got a car not far from here . . ."

At that hour, the avenue was deserted and

silent. You could hear the rustling of trees. The more we walked, the more we were lit only by the full moon. At least, as I remember it.

In front of the Schmidt villa, an American convertible was parked along the sidewalk. I immediately recognized it. That same day, I'd seen it parked on Rue Royale.

"The owner always leaves the key on the dashboard."

He opened the door and signaled me to get in. I hesitated.

"Don't be scared," Daniel V. said. "He'll never know."

I sat in the front seat and Daniel V. slammed the door shut. It was too late to back out.

Daniel V. settled behind the wheel. He turned the ignition and I heard the particular sound of American engines that had so impressed me ever since childhood, because they made you feel like you were about to lift off the ground.

We drove by the police station and followed the road that skirted the lake. I kept expecting a squad car to come rushing out.

"You don't seem very relaxed," said Daniel V. "Take it easy . . . I know this guy's schedule by heart. He never goes to his car before three in the morning. He gambles at the casino."

"But why does he leave the key on the dash-board?"

"The car is registered in Italy, in Rome . . . Leaving the key on the dash must be what they do there."

"But what if somebody asks for your driver's license?"

"I'll just say the guy lent me his car. We can always work it out with him."

Daniel V. ended up communicating his non-chalance to me. After all, I wasn't even seventeen yet.

"The last time I borrowed this car, I went as far as La Clusaz . . ."

He drove slowly and I no longer heard the motor. I felt a very slight pitching, as if we were skimming a lake.

"I don't know the guy . . . but he was born around here . . . He comes back to Annecy now and then in the summer . . . I spotted him two years ago because of his car . . . His name is Serge Servoz . . ."

He opened the glove compartment and handed me a driver's license bearing that name, along with the photo of a man who was still young but seemed much older than us. In the following days and months, I realized that the name "Serge Servoz" had stuck in my memory.

"Tonight, we can drive it all the way to Geneva," said Daniel V. "What do you say?"

But he must have read the alarm in my eyes, as he patted my knee.

"Take it easy . . . I'm only joking . . ."

He had slowed down still further and the car glided in silence, as if coasting. The empty avenue ahead and the moon's reflections on the lake. After Chavoire, I stopped worrying. It now felt as if this car belonged to us.

"Tomorrow night, same time, we can go for another ride," said Daniel V.

"Do you think the car will be parked in the same place?"

"Either there or in front of the police station. During the day, he always parks along the arcades, in the first street to the right after the Taverne."

I was astounded at such precision. We had arrived at Veyrier-du-Lac and gone past the large plane tree that marked the bus stop, the one I took on Sunday evenings to return to boarding school.

He cut the motor just as he passed through the open gateway to "The Lindens," and the car coasted down the sloping driveway to the front door of the house.

"Next time, we'll go to Geneva."

He reversed up the drive and waved his arm in farewell.

I would see him again in November of the following year, one Sunday when I was returning to school. That evening, when I boarded the bus at Veyrier-du-Lac, there were no free seats. I stood alongside other passengers. He was standing too, right near me, in uniform.

"Yup, it's me," he said with a sheepish smile. "I'm doing my military service in Annecy."

And he told me he'd gotten married to a girl who was expecting their first child in several months and they were living at his in-laws' in the little village of Alex. He'd gotten permission from the military authorities to go home at night.

He looked different because of his crew cut and especially, I felt, the sadness in his eyes.

"And you?" he asked. "Still studying away?"

"Still studying."

I didn't know what else to say to him.

Before the bus stopped in the village of Alex, he gripped my arm:

"All in all, we were better off in Serge Servoz's convertible than in this bus, don't you think?"

And as if he were trying to convince himself, he told me he hadn't given up on his plan to work in the hotel industry abroad. Not in Geneva, it was too nearby. But maybe London.

Trying to bring my research up to date, I get a very strange feeling. It's as if all this was already written in invisible ink. How does the dictionary define it? "Ink, colorless when first used, that darkens when treated with a given substance." Perhaps, at the turn of a page, what was set down in invisible ink will gradually emerge, and the questions I've been asking myself for so long about Noëlle Lefebvre's disappearance, as well as the reason I've been asking myself those questions, will be resolved with the precision and clarity of a police report. In a neat hand that looks like mine, explanations will be provided in minutest detail, the mysteries cleared up. And perhaps this will allow me, once and for all, to better understand myself.

The idea of invisible ink came to me a few days ago, as I was again leafing through Noëlle Lefebvre's datebook. On the page for July 2: "Saw Sancho again at La Caravelle, Rue Robert-Estienne. I should never have gone back to that place. Now what?" I was certain I hadn't read that before and that the page had been blank. These words were in blue ink, a blue that was much paler than the other notes, almost translucent. And, studying the other blank pages of the datebook closely and under bright light, I seemed to see traces of writing, like watermarks, but it was impossible to make out the letters or words. It appeared to be the same for every page, as if she had kept a daily log or recorded a large number of appointments. I looked into that "given substance" the dictionary mentioned. No doubt a product commonly found in stores, thanks to which everything Noëlle Lefebvre jotted down in her datebook will rise to the surface of the white page, as if she had written it the day before. Or else it will all happen naturally, turn legible overnight. It's only a matter of time.

The proof: it took me decades to learn that I'd been mistaken about the spelling of the name "Behaviour."

I had only heard it from Gérard Mourade and was convinced it should be written the English way: Behaviour. But no. I realized my error fifteen years ago, as I was walking along the quay toward the head offices of Radio France.

I had arrived at the large garage just before the elevated metro tracks and the stairways of Rue de l'Alboni. Above the garage entrance, a white sign bore this inscription in red letters:

TROCADÉRO GARAGE
R. Béavioure
Specializing in Chryslers
24-hour service

I knew this neighborhood well and was amazed I'd never noticed that sign, and especially the name BÉAVIOURE. But perhaps you had to wait for time to pass before letters and names appeared, like on the pages of Noëlle Lefebvre's datebook. It comforted me to think that even if you sometimes have memory gaps, all the details of your life are written somewhere in invisible ink.

Through the large glass partition, I saw a man seated at a metal desk, head bent over, ap-

parently reading through a file. I knocked on
the partition. He looked up and motioned me
to come in.

I was standing, facing him. A man in his
early fifties, white hair in a brush-cut, something
childlike about his face, probably due to his gaze
and the smooth, tan skin that contrasted with his
white hair.

"How can I help you, sir?"

His voice, too, was childlike, with a slight
Paris accent.

"Are you Roger Béavioure?"

"I am."

"I just needed some information . . ."

He was wearing a navy blue cotton jacket and
yellow polo shirt that gave him an athletic look.

"At your service . . ."

He smiled at me, with a smile that no doubt
hadn't changed since he was young. I was afraid
that smile would freeze when I came to the point.

"It's about your name . . ."

"My name?"

He knit his brow, and his smile faded.

"I believe you might have known, a long time ago, some friends of mine . . ."

The sentence struck me as rather blunt, but I had said it very gently.

"Friends? What friends?"

"A girl named Noëlle Lefebvre and a boy who was called Gérard Mourade. I'm talking about quite some time ago . . . I think you and I are about the same age . . ."

I had expressed it as carefully as I could to gain his confidence, doing my best to sound casual. But I sensed his apprehension.

His look had darkened and he kept silent. I wondered whether what I'd just said unnerved him or whether he was trying to remember.

"Could you please repeat those names?"

"Gérard Mourade and Noëlle Lefebvre. Noëlle Lefebvre disappeared without warning. I knew she was living with a certain Roger Béavioure . . ."

"The first name doesn't ring any bells. But I did know a girl named Noëlle. It was ages ago . . ."

"I suppose that's the same girl," I said. "At the time, she lived on Rue Vaugelas."

"No, *I* lived on Rue Vaugelas. She lived on Rue de la Convention."

He gave a brief nod, as if wanting to put an end to the conversation.

"You never found out what had become of Noëlle Lefebvre?"

"No."

He stared steadily at me. He seemed to be searching for words.

"You say she disappeared. But she simply left Paris, if I remember correctly."

The telephone on his desk rang at that moment. He picked up the receiver.

"I'm with a customer . . . Why don't you come meet me here . . ."

He hung up.

"You see, there are parts of the past that we would rather forget . . . And so we blank them out . . . And that's just fine . . . I had a rocky start in life . . ."

He was smiling, but his smile had become tense.

"I understand," I told him. "I had a rocky start in life, too. And we both knew the same person. It's not just a coincidence . . ."

"It's nothing *but* a coincidence, sir."

His tone was much less friendly than before.

"You're talking about such a long time ago . . . And about someone I knew for a very short while . . . Barely three months . . . I'm not sure what else I can say to you."

He might have been telling the truth. Three months is nothing in a lifetime. And, after all those years, Noëlle Lefebvre was no more to him than a bit player in a film on cloudy stock, one of those bit players whose face you don't even see, only her outline, from behind, in the background.

"I understand perfectly . . . And I apologize for having bothered you."

He seemed surprised by those words, which I

had no doubt uttered in sorrowful tones. I felt he wanted to do a little more for me. Professional reflex? After all, I was a customer—he'd said so on the phone.

"But why are you looking for her? Was Noëlle important to you?"

It was the first time he'd said her name as if speaking of a loved one.

"I'm merely trying to find out why she disappeared."

At that moment, a woman entered the office, a redhead, wearing a suede jacket and beige slacks, a good twenty years younger than Béavioure. She greeted me with a slight nod.

"Will you be much longer?"

"No," said Béavioure, looking embarrassed. "The gentleman and I were just talking cars. He's a connoisseur."

He turned to me.

"My wife."

She gave me a distracted glance.

"I'll do my best to find you that model, sir,"

Béavioure said, taking me by the arm and guiding me to the door of his office. "Of course, there aren't many Chrysler Valiants on the market. But I feel confident."

We were both outside, on the quay. He leaned toward me.

"Before, you said the name 'Mourade.' I think I did know someone by that name . . ."

It was as if he wanted to confide in me.

"He lived with me for a short while, on Rue Vaugelas . . . He was unbalanced . . . He used to make up the most outlandish stories . . . He even turned himself in to the police once, claiming he'd killed someone . . ."

The words poured from his mouth faster and faster, as if he feared being interrupted.

"What else can I tell you about Noëlle? I don't know . . ."

He cast a worried glance at the garage. Perhaps he was afraid his wife would suddenly appear.

"I met Noëlle when she first came to Paris . . . She was from the provinces . . . some mountain range or other . . . She was married to a man who was older than her . . . I was young, and the thing that impressed me was this guy had an American convertible. And guess what make? A Chrysler."

He held out his hand.

"So long, sir . . . I'd rather not think about those days anymore . . . I managed to get out in one piece . . . but just barely . . ."

I walked up the stairs of Rue de l'Alboni toward the metro stop. I had again been naïve to think Béavioure would tell me everything about Noëlle Lefebvre and help me understand why I'd been interested in her for so long. And I ended up believing that I was seeking a missing link in my own life.

Instead of taking the metro, I turned into Passage des Eaux, a place that, in fact, reminded me of certain episodes in my life. I had long been convinced that, on this path, sooner or later, I would run into people I'd once known. To the right were windows, but you couldn't tell which buildings they belonged to, any more than you could know where the front doors of those buildings might be found. You just had to tap on the panes and a face would appear, a face you hadn't seen in thirty years and might have forgotten— and that face would not have changed. Several people, whose fates you wondered about, resided there, in ground-floor rooms, sheltered from time. They would open their windows for you. The passage was deserted and silent, as usual. To the left, a surrounding wall, behind which might have been a park or the edge of a wood. Farther on, at the end of the walk, a silhouette was coming forward, down the slope, and we were about to cross paths. Noëlle Lefebvre? I thought about the sign on the quay and its red lettering—"Trocadéro Garage. R. Béavioure. Specializing in Chryslers. 24-hour service"—and I felt like laughing. You can never trust witnesses. Their supposed statements about the people they knew are usually faulty, and all they do is muddy the waters. The outlines of a life disappear behind all that muddying. How can we ever disentangle the true from the false, given all the conflicting traces a person leaves behind? And do we know any more about ourselves, judging by my own lies and omissions, or my involuntary lapses?

The silhouette came closer, holding a small boy by the hand. As they passed by, I almost asked if her name was Noëlle Lefebvre. But did she even know, or had she forgotten? I couldn't help gazing after them until they had disappeared past the entrance of Passage des Eaux.

This investigation might give the impression that I've devoted considerable time to it—already more than a hundred pages—but that isn't quite true. If one were to put end to end the moments I've haphazardly evoked so far, they would add up to barely a day. What is one day over a span of thirty years? And thirty years had elapsed between the spring when Hutte sent me to the General Delivery window and my conversation with Roger Béavioure, whose name was not spelled Behaviour. In short, thirty years during which Noëlle Lefebvre had not truly occupied my mind for more than one day.

That thought needed visit me only for a few hours, or even a few minutes, for it to assume its importance. In the fairly rectilinear track of my life, she was a question that had remained unanswered. And if I continue to write this book, it's only in the possibly vain hope of finding an answer. I wonder—must I really find an answer? I'm afraid that once you have all the answers, your life closes in on you like a trap, with the clank of keys in a prison cell. Wouldn't it be better to leave empty lots around you, into which you can escape?

But for the file to be as complete as possible, I have to mention a very brief episode — so brief that, afterward, I doubted its reality and wondered more than once whether it didn't belong to the realm of dreams.

It was in the month of June, one evening around eleven in the pharmacy on Place Blanche. Two men were in front of me, and one of them, the shorter one, had handed the pharmacist a prescription. The larger one was leaning on the other's shoulder, as if having difficulty standing upright. Despite his corpulence and his overly dyed blond hair, he who'd been dark some fifteen years earlier, I thought I recognized Gérard Mourade. He was wearing a striped polo shirt. My impression was confirmed when I moved next to him. His face was the same as before, except that his cheeks were puffier. Our eyes met.

When they left the pharmacy, the man in whom I'd recognized Gérard Mourade was still leaning on his friend's shoulder, and I followed behind.

They were walking on Boulevard de Clichy, along the median strip. I caught up with them.

"Excuse me . . . Aren't you Gérard Mourade?"

He hadn't heard. The other one turned toward me.

"Can we help you?"

A fairly young brunet, with the dark, apprehensive eyes of certain terriers.

He placed himself between Mourade and me, as if he were his bodyguard and meant to protect him.

"Is this gentleman Gérard Mourade?"

"No. I'm afraid you're mistaken."

Mourade hung back, looking toward us indifferently.

"What's going on, Folco?" he asked in a very soft voice.

"Nothing," said the little brunet. "The gentleman mistook you for someone else."

"Ah, I see . . . He's mistaken me for someone else, has he?"

He had a vague smile.

"This man's name is André Vernet, not Gérard Mourade," the little brunet said in a cutting voice.

"Ask him if he remembers Noëlle Lefebvre . . ."

He whispered into Mourade's ear, and the latter shook his head. The little brunet came back toward me.

"He has no recollection whatsoever of that person."

And once again, Mourade—or Vernet— rested his hand on the other's shoulder and they walked slowly to a gray Volkswagen parked alongside the median. The little brunet opened the passenger door and helped Mourade—or

Vernet—to settle in. I watched them from a distance.

The car, with the one called Folco at the wheel, drove past me toward Pigalle, then I saw it disappear forever. Perhaps I should have jotted down the numbers and letters on the license plate.

I had received a letter from Jacques B., aka "the Marquis," no doubt a few weeks after our meeting at Richelieu-Drouot. The letter wasn't dated, and that is of no importance. I have never respected chronological order. It has never existed for me. Present and past blend together in a kind of transparency, and every instant I lived in my youth appears to me in an eternal present, set apart from everything.

Jacques B., aka "the Marquis," wrote:

My dear Jean,

When we saw each other, I asked for the names of people you knew were connected with Noëlle Lefebvre. I jotted them down, thinking I might find a few clues to help with your search.

You mentioned a Gérard Mourade. In the archives of my newspaper, I discovered an item about him from five years ago. A human interest piece, my specialty. A strange "case" that was never followed up—there's no further mention of it, so it must have been considered closed . . .

Jacques B. had attached a photocopy of the article:

KIDNAPPED ACTOR KILLS CAPTOR

Last Ascension Thursday, a man named André Vernet, residing at 26 Rue Carnot in Maisons-Alfort, who also goes by the stage name Gérard Mourade, turned himself in to the police station at Gare d'Austerlitz, claiming he had just killed a man on Rue de l'Essai.

This being verified, André Vernet was charged with voluntary homicide and interrogated by the examining magistrate, Mr. Marquiset, in the presence of his lawyer, Mr. Mariani.

The accused then gave a rather burlesque account of his misadventures.

On an unspecified pretext [Jacques B. had underlined those words and added in ballpoint pen: "what pretext?"], he was lured on May 11 to 19 Rue Béranger, where he was then surrounded by six individuals who robbed him of his papers, money, and the jewelry he was wearing. [Jacques B. had added in ballpoint: "Why jewelry?"] Four days later, he was taken to Rue de l'Essai; on the night of the 17th, as he was being guarded by only two men, then by just one, he managed to overpower his captor, killing him in the ensuing struggle.

Jacques B.'s letter continued:

*I suppose this Mourade was forced to give up the theater
. . . Perhaps he left some traces behind in Maisons-Alfort?*

*As for Sancho Lefebvre, I was able to get some informa-
tion from reliable sources in Annecy.*

*His real name is Serge Servoz-Lefebvre, aka "Sancho
Lefebvre," born in Annecy on September 6, 1932. In adolescence and young adulthood, he worked in various hotels
in Annecy and Megève. In Megève, he met a fellow named
Georges Brainos and became his secretary, then his business partner. The latter owned movie theaters in Brussels
and Geneva and a company that managed two establish-
ments in Paris: the La Marine Dance Club at 71 Quai de
Grenelle (15th), and the restaurant La Caravelle at 26 Rue
Marbeuf–2 Rue Robert-Estienne (8th). Sancho Lefebvre
was involved in these businesses.*

He apparently lived in Switzerland and Rome.

*On August 4, 1962, he was stopped at the French bor-
der, coming from Switzerland, and in the trunk of his car
they found a painting by Henri Matisse belonging to a
Mme Charlotte Wendland (Versoix, Canton of Geneva)
that she'd given him to sell. His official papers make no
mention of a marriage.*

*Nonetheless, in the summer of '63 or '64, he was seen
in Annecy with a young woman whose name was in fact
Noëlle, whom he introduced as his wife. I checked with some*

*friends who are older than us, who you no doubt remember
(Claude Brun, Paulo Hervieu, Guy Pilotaz), and they confirmed this. She called herself "Mme Lefebvre." But they
didn't know anything about her and couldn't think of anyone
else who might. According to them, she was born somewhere
in the region. After that summer of '63 or '64, neither Serge
Servoz-Lefebvre, aka "Sancho," nor "Mme" Lefebvre was
seen again in Annecy.*

*There you have it, my dear Jean. Who knows? I might
get some more information to send you. Until then, best of
luck,*

JACQUES

Yes, best of luck. Despite his efforts, Jacques B.
hadn't managed to identify "Mme Lefebvre."
"According to them, she was born somewhere in
the region." There, too, we're still in the dark.
What were the parameters of that region? Annecy?
Chambéry? Thonon-les-Bains? Geneva? As for
Claude Brun, Paulo Hervieu, and Guy Pilotaz, they "didn't know anything about her" and
"couldn't think of anyone else who might" . . .

I went to put Jacques B.'s letter in the file. It
already contained so many details, like paths in a

forest that you follow at random, making choices at every intersection, and that lead you farther and farther astray as daylight wanes. Or the rare and faded memories you might have of someone, knowing nothing about the rest of that person's life. What was the only tangible element in this file? An underdeveloped photo on a General Delivery ID card, a face in black and white that you would barely have recognized in the street . . . All the supplemental details that I might still have gathered reminded me of the crackling of static in a telephone, growing louder and louder. It keeps you from hearing a voice calling to you from far away.

She told herself it might have been an illusion, but there seemed to be far fewer Frenchmen in Rome than before. Not tourists, but those French who, by the time she arrived in Rome, had lived there for a decade or so. Others had settled there at around the same time as she and were her age, but that afternoon she was thinking about the older ones, whose names resurfaced in her memory: Gallas, Cressoy, Sernas, Georges Brehat; and women, too: Corey, Andreu, Hélène Remy . . . You often ran into them in the same places; they were recognizable from their way of speaking a mix of French and Italian, a mix that had gradually become a new language, a kind of Esperanto. But for what mysterious reasons would someone decide to go into exile in Rome? Exile from what? Apparently, all of them had blotted out the first part of their life, the part they'd lived in France. Rome was a city that had the power to erase time, as well as one's past, like the Foreign Legion. No doubt she owed these reflections to the man who had come earlier to the gallery on Via della Scrofa. A man her age, French.

She had seen him stop in front of the display window and read the sign on the door: "Gaspard of the Night." It was the nickname of a friend of hers, an Italian who managed that gallery, where he gathered and exhibited the many photos he'd taken of Rome's night life at a certain period. He was away for two months and had asked her to fill in for him.

He had hesitated to go inside, then had opened the door with a determined movement, as if taking the plunge. He had greeted her with a nod and examined the photos displayed on the walls one by one.

She was sitting at the small desk. He walked up to her:

"Are you French?"

"Yes."

"Have you been in Rome a long time?"

"Since forever."

She was speaking the truth. She had the impression she'd been born here and that the events preceding her arrival were those of a former life, of which she kept only vague recollections.

"Was it you who came up with 'Gaspard of the Night'?"

He had asked the question with a slight Parisian accent, smiling.

"No, it was the owner. A former photographer who usually worked after dark."

"Very interesting pictures . . . Are they for sale?"

"Of course. And there are many more not on view, which you can see in the storage back there . . ."

She pointed to a small door at the rear of the gallery. And she suddenly wondered if the word "storage" was correct, as she had lost the habit of conversing in her native tongue.

"I'd love to see them."

He didn't know what more to say. She, too, kept silent.

"Could I know the photographer's name?"

"Gaspard Mugnani. Here's a book of his work, if you're interested."

And she handed him a copy of the photo album on her desk.

He began leafing through it. Nocturnal views of the streets and squares of Rome, empty, or animated like the Via Veneto back in its heyday, with its summer holiday terraces and its regulars, whose names were mentioned at the bottom of the page. Black-and-white photos, plus a few in bright neon colors.

"They should have added some sort of explanatory text to go with these photos, don't you think?"

She was surprised at how carefully he was studying them.

"You should talk to the photographer about that. He's away at the moment, but he'll be back next month."

She gave him an ironic smile, as he seemed increasingly absorbed by those photos.

"So are you managing the gallery while he's away?"

"Yes. But there aren't many customers. Sometimes I only come in every other day."

He continued leafing through the album.

"If you've been in Rome a long time, I suppose you know all the people in these photographs."

And he showed her two pages featuring black-and-white images of various individuals, taken at night on Via Veneto—as the caption indicated.

He had moved closer to her and held the book open so she could get a better look at those two pages.

"Yes, I knew them all by sight, pretty much. It was around the time I first moved to Rome. Most of them are dead now."

Truth be told, she had never looked through the album. And the photos hanging on the walls she must have glanced at once, distractedly.

"And what about you," she asked, "do you live in Rome?"

He could have been one of those Frenchmen around her age who'd come to the city and settled there permanently. Many of them were still alive.

"No. I'll be here for a few days, just long enough to do some research for a study I plan to write."

"Are you a professor?"

"Sure. Professor."

He shut the album and held it in his hand.

"Would you let me borrow this?"

"Yes, gladly."

From his way of speaking, his movements, she suddenly had the impression she'd seen him somewhere before.

"Do you come to Rome often?"

"No. Never. I live in Paris."

She'd been mistaken. And yet, looking more closely at him, he might have lived in Rome. What made her think that? She couldn't explain it. Perhaps his eyes, the timbre of his voice.

"I'll bring you back the album tomorrow, if you're here. I might have some questions for you about life in Rome."

Why life in Rome? She preferred not to ask immediately.

"Come tomorrow at the same time. I'm never here in the morning."

He gently closed the glass door behind him. She thought to herself that he held the album in his hand like a schoolboy with his satchel.

That evening, the air was not as warm as usual. Autumn already. Leaving the gallery, she decided to walk up to Via Flaminia, where she was to meet a friend. She was very early for their appointment, and it would allow her to make a detour that reminded her of the long walks she used to take during her first visit to the city. Back then she would try to retain the names of the streets and squares, but each time she forgot them and would end up getting lost.

So he was looking for information about "life in Rome" . . . But what did he mean by that? She'd been walking at random for some time when she noticed she was following the arcades of Piazza Esedra, and she was amazed she'd gone so far, as if she'd covered the whole route while sleepwalking and had only just awakened. She now knew the city so well that she could no longer get lost, and she regretted it.

Never again would there be anything new for her here, and before long she'd be able to walk from place to place with eyes closed. She'd need only to count her steps, the number of which would remain constant between the Gaspard of the Night gallery and the Piazza del Popolo.

Maybe, when you thought about it, that's what "life in Rome" was: a metronomic tick-tock, regular and eternal, and also pointless, since time had stopped forever.

She found herself at the start of the Via Veneto, and she wondered whether, when leaving the gallery, it was here that she'd meant to guide her steps, or rather let herself be guided by them. A neighborhood she had known well when she'd first lived in Rome. The café terraces spilling out onto the sidewalk had still been shaded at the time by parasols in every color. And then, as the years passed, there had been less and less bustle on the avenue, evidence that the younger crowd preferred other parts of town. Or else, the people you used to see in summer, on the terraces or slowly cruising by in convertibles looking for late-night companions, had gradually died out.

Night was falling. She walked up the avenue, which looked darker than on other evenings. A power outage? Unless the streetlamps weren't yet lit at that twilight hour. She walked by the Café de Paris. It was closed. A metal gate with a padlock protected the door and, behind the gate, on the front step, lay a heap of old flyers, newspapers, letters, leaflets, empty plastic bottles, as if no one had crossed that threshold in an eternity. A little farther up, on the right, the massive Excelsior hotel. A lone light in a top-floor window. Farther on, the façade of the Doney tearoom, dark.

She encountered no one on the avenue. Gaspard of the Night should have taken a photo of the Via Veneto, empty at that hour, and put it at the end of his album. It would have contrasted sharply with the preceding images, and so one would have felt the passage of time. She'd mention it when she saw him next.

The passage of time. She had always lived in the present, so that the path of her life was riddled with gaps in her memory. She couldn't say whether they were actual lapses or whether she avoided thinking about certain events. She had a son who had gone to America. Did she regret not having started a family? But what exactly was a family? She was born in a village and into a family, yet she would have been incapable of answering that question.

Her life was now a long story, too long, that she would have recounted to someone who could gain her trust. But who? And why? So all that remained to her was the present with its reference points, several fixed, immutable images: the pine tree in Piazza Pitagora that she saw from her windows; the dead leaves of the plane trees, every autumn, on the banks of the Tiber.

And besides, did it really exist, the passage of time, in that city they called eternal? Of course, as the years drifted by, people disappeared, lights went out, silence fell in places where one was used to hearing boisterous conversations and loud laughter. And despite all that, there was something eternal in the air. That was what she could explain tomorrow to that man who wanted information about "life in Rome." But would she find the words? The simplest thing, if he wanted to understand her state of mind since she'd been living here, would be to recite a poem, the only one she knew more or less by heart:

The sky is, above the roof,
So calm, so fair!
A branch, above the roof,
Fans the air

And the idea made her burst out with a laugh whose echo she thought she could hear up and down the deserted avenue.

She had copied down that poem long ago, in the previous century, in a datebook. It was during her very short stay in Paris, before leaving for Rome. That stay, which had lasted only a few months, had gradually faded from her memory. The few months had become a few hours, as if she had spent them in a waiting room between two trains. She recalled no faces, not even the name of the street she had lived on. The train was rolling too fast for her to read the names of the stations on the platform signs. If she'd been able to hold onto that datebook—the only one she'd ever kept in her life—and if she leafed through it today, would the appointments, the places, the names still mean anything to her? She wasn't sure. Someone had stolen the date-book from her: a large fellow, whose face and name she'd forgotten, someone she'd met with a friend of his in a café. They both lived in the same neighborhood as she and they'd seen each other once or twice, but it had meant no more than if they were two anonymous neighbors with whom she exchanged a few words lost forever in the mists of time.

The large fellow, as a joke, had snatched away the datebook, in which she'd just jotted down an appointment, and refused to give it back. After that, she had left for Rome without reclaiming it. Two trivial details had nonethe-less stuck in her memory: that faceless, nameless man wore waffle-weave shirts under a sheepskin jacket. And he was taking acting lessons. And his friend, who was always with him, also remained nameless and faceless. The only thing she remembered about him was that he worked for a moving company.

She had arrived at Via Aurora, near the Maronite church. Each time she passed by the spot, she felt a slight pang. When she was nineteen, she had often ended up on Via Aurora after a night out. At the beginning of the street, a high wall above which one could make out a garden that must have belonged to the Aurora Casino. And that wall, in summer, at around six in the morning, was already spattered with sunlight. A table and chair were always set out on the sidewalk, at the foot of the wall. She would sit there, in the sun, the morning sun that was still very gentle. Over the years, and even this evening when everything around her was so dark, she felt as if that sunlight had never left her, and was now enveloping her in a kind of aurora borealis.

A little farther up the avenue, on the window of the English shoe shop Luciano Padovan, someone had posted a flyer dated the previous

October: a lost-and-found notice, with photo, for a dog that had gone missing in the area around Piazzale Flaminio. She read it start to finish:

> Small dog named Greta, missing as of 10/17 on Via Gian Domenico Romagnosi. If found, please call: Italian International Film, 063611377. She is wearing a red collar. Breed: smooth-coat dachshund.

She had never noticed this lost-and-found flyer, which must also have been posted in other streets around there. When she had finished reading, she thought about the Frenchman to whom she'd lent Gaspard of the Night's album. For some reason, she pictured him with a dog.

"A very interesting album . . ."

He was holding it in his hand and had taken a seat on the red sofa in the "storage," as she called it: an annex to the gallery, whose half-open French doors offered a view of a sunlit courtyard. She sat facing him in a leather armchair.

"I'm more and more convinced that there should be some kind of text here . . ."

She didn't dare ask what kind of text one might write about Gaspard of the Night's photographs. Those photos depicted places and people that were familiar to her and had in a way been part of her daily routine, such that a "text" seemed redundant.

"So if I understand correctly, you're very interested in Rome?"

She hadn't been able to say it without a slight smirk.

"Very. But for someone like you who's been here a long time, that must seem simple tourist curiosity . . ."

That was exactly what she would have said. So they understood each other.

"This city is so different from Paris . . ."

She had said it without thinking, just to break the silence.

"Have you lived in Paris?"

"Oh . . . only for a few months . . . a long time ago. And I'm ashamed to admit it, but I remember almost nothing about the place . . ."

"Really?"

He suddenly seemed disappointed that she should remember so little, or that she should display such nonchalance or levity.

"I don't know if you've noticed, but I speak French with an Italian accent . . . and often I find it hard to speak French at all . . ."

"I apologize for putting you through the effort."

For his part, he spoke meticulous French, with his Parisian accent.

"I'm very interested in French people, or any other foreigners, who settled in Rome during the twentieth century. I think there might be a book in it."

"So are you a history professor?"

"Exactly. I'm a history professor."

He had said it with an air of self-mockery, and of not wanting to divulge other details about his work. But that didn't bother her. In Rome, you never asked new acquaintances indiscreet questions about their professional or personal lives. You accepted them tacitly, as if you had known them forever. You guessed everything about them without having to ask.

"So, you honestly liked Gaspard's album?"

She wasn't quite sure how to jump-start the conversation. He seemed to be preoccupied by something. Or else to be thinking how best to phrase a question he wanted to ask.

"It interested me enormously. I recognized several people in those photos. But you must know them better than I do, in any case . . ."

He leafed through the album slowly, as he had the day before. She wondered whether he

would take much longer. Apparently he had forgotten she was there. He halted on a page.

"There's a man in this photo who has a
French name . . . But I can't imagine who he
might be . . ."

He showed her a photo of three people seated
at an outdoor café table. A black-and-white
photo, taken on a summer evening judging from
their outfits—beachwear. Underneath, the caption read, "Left to right: Duccio Staderini, Sancho Lefebvre, Giorgio Costa."

She leaned in toward the photo.

"Which one are you interested in?"

"The one in the middle, with the French
name . . . Sancho Lefebvre . . ."

She remained there, leaning over the photo,
not speaking. She didn't know if she was reluc-
tant to answer or if those faces really meant
nothing to her, as if she had been stricken by
sudden amnesia.

"Sancho Lefebvre? Yes, he was French . . .
His real name wasn't Sancho, but Serge . . ."

"Did you know him?"

"A little. When I first came to Rome, at nineteen."

And it was curious, but at first glance she hadn't recognized him in the photo: a dark-haired man, much taller than the other two, and the only one not smiling. And then something clicked into place, and she found herself back in the skin of the young woman who had known Serge, aka Sancho, Lefebvre. But it lasted only a few seconds. The photo again became the one of her first glance, and he someone who was now so distant . . .

"And do you know how he made his living or why he was in Rome?"

"I never asked that sort of question. I would run into him now and again, as I did most of the French who lived here."

She didn't want to go into detail. Moreover, the details had grown blurred. No more handholds. Amnesia had covered it all with a glassy white blanket. With snow.

"Yesterday, you said you'd like some information about Rome . . . What kind of information?"

She was having trouble finding her words. She felt as if she no longer knew how to speak French. The phrases refused to come. She had to try harder.

"It's very difficult . . . In Rome, you gradually end up forgetting everything . . ."

Yes, she had read that reflection somewhere. In a crime novel or a magazine. Rome was the city of forgetting.

She stood up suddenly from the leather armchair.

"Would you like to take a walk outside? It's stifling in this storage . . ."

He seemed surprised. No doubt because of the word "storage," and she again wondered if it was the correct term.

They followed Via della Scrofa, walking side by side, he still holding the album.

"It must be boring for you to sit in that gallery all day . . ."

"Oh, you know, I only spend two hours a day there . . ."

"Do you live around here?"

"Not very far. And what about you, are you in a hotel?"

"Yes. Near the Piazza del Popolo."

The conversation became banal and undemanding. You just had to float on your back. But something was nagging at her.

"Why are you so interested in Sancho Lefebvre?"

How many years had it been since she'd spoken that name? Since the previous century, probably. And it made her feel uneasy.

"Someone in Paris mentioned him in conversation . . . The name Sancho had struck me . . ."

He turned to her and smiled as if in reassurance. Reassurance? She might take his smile the wrong way.

"Yes . . . Someone who apparently knew this Sancho Lefebvre, a long time ago . . ."

He had stopped in the middle of the sidewalk, looking as if he wanted to tell her something important.

"Sometimes you find yourself in a place among people, most of whom you don't know . . . and all you can do is listen to their conversations . . ."

She didn't really understand what he was driving at, but she nodded in agreement.

"It was during one of those chance conversations that I heard the name Sancho Lefebvre . . . And there you have it . . . it's as simple as that . . . and as inane . . . and then I find his picture in your album . . ."

He took her arm and they continued walking. They arrived at Piazza del Popolo.

"The person who mentioned Sancho Lefebvre in that conversation was an older man, but his hair was still dark; he looked like he might have been Greek or South American . . ."

She studied him curiously, and then she too smiled.

"It's like a whole novel, what you're telling me . . ."

"Yes, you're right . . . a novel . . . That man had apparently been a friend of Sancho Lefebvre's . . . His name was Brainos. Georges Brainos."

This time, it was she who stopped in the middle of the plaza. Brainos. A name she had forgotten for decades, that she had not heard mentioned since that time, by anyone. Which is why the name surged from oblivion with some violence. But she couldn't put a face to it, as if the two syllables, "Brai-nos," shone a blinding light on her.

"You look pale . . . Perhaps the walk has tired you out . . . and I get the feeling I'm boring you with all this . . ."

"No, not at all . . . Why don't we go sit somewhere?"

She had just experienced a slight dizziness,

but was feeling better. The name "Brainos" had already become a blinking light, growing ever dimmer, as when you pull away from shore.

How old would this Brainos be today, assuming he was still alive? A hundred? She was tempted to ask him, since he had met the man, or so he said. "He looked like he might have been Greek or South American." Of his face, all that she remembered was his dark, slicked-back hair. And black eyes.

They were sitting next to each other at a sidewalk table at Rosati.

"No . . . I've never heard of this Brainos . . . I never knew anyone by that name in Rome."

She felt bad about lying. Why not tell him the truth? While the man had become faceless for her, the particular sound of his name evoked something. She suddenly thought of those two young people, a girl and a boy, whose intact bodies had been found preserved in a glacier, fifty years after their death, near the village in Haute-Savoie where she was born. Memories, too, had remained buried in ice, and all it had

taken was the name Brainos to make them re-
surface, even if a bit obscured by time. She
wondered whether she had met Brainos before
Sancho Lefebvre, or whether it was Sancho Lefebvre who had introduced her to Brainos. It
seemed to her she had met both of them one
summer, at the Grand Hôtel de Menthon-Saint-
Bernard where she was working. In any case, it
was Sancho Lefebvre who had persuaded her to
leave "her province," as he put it, as he himself
had done a few years earlier. And she had also
decided, that summer, to change her name. But
why had she picked Noëlle?

She recalled a small chateau in Sologne—
"Brainos's castle in Sologne," Sancho Lefebvre often repeated as if it were the refrain of an
old French song, apparently poking fun at Brainos—a "castle" where she had spent several
weeks with Sancho Lefebvre and Brainos.

"Really, I get the impression you're writing a
novel right now, given all the people with curious names that you're interested in . . ."

She did her best to keep her tone playful, but

she felt ill at ease. For the first time, these memories were visiting her, like a blackmailer whom
you were sure had lost track of you long ago, and
who, one evening, knocks softly at your door.

"Yes, you're right . . . a novel . . ."

He shrugged and gave her a smile.

"They told me about a Frenchwoman living
in Rome . . . They had a nickname for her, long
ago . . . 'the Shepherdess of the Alps' . . . Does
that ring any bells?"

"No."

"And how come you decided to settle in
Rome permanently?"

"Just by chance."

She could find no other word for it. She had
never stopped to ask, but since she was now delv-
ing back into the past because of those names
abruptly ripped from the shadows—Sancho Lefebvre, Brainos—she wondered what her state
of mind had been back then. Well, quite simply,
escape was her modus operandi at the time. First
escaping from the place where she was born.
Then escaping from Serge aka Sancho Lefeb-

vre, not long after meeting him and living with him in Rome. Hiding out in Paris. And after Serge aka Sancho Lefebvre had found her, running away with him back to Rome. And, after his death, staying in this city, in a kind of permanent escape. An endless escape.

"Yes, chance. Just chance . . ."

After all, she had no reason to confide in this man. For that, they would have to know each other better.

"So will you be going back to Paris soon?"

"Not immediately."

"Be careful. If you linger in Rome too long, you risk staying here forever."

The conversation had again taken a trivial turn, and she felt relieved. The shadows of Sancho Lefebvre and Brainos had dissipated. But after a few moments, she felt some discomfort. Why had he alluded to those two people, both of whom were related to a period in her life— a period so distant that she never thought about it anymore? One photo among hundreds of others in an album, a name uttered by a phantom one evening, in the buzz of conversation—how could such vague details have caught his attention? She must not have been entirely unknown to him; someone must have mentioned her. Otherwise, how could she explain these coincidences? She decided to ask.

She turned toward him. He was contemplating the plaza, the twin churches and the obelisk. Night had fallen and the café was about to close. And yet, it seemed perfectly natural for the two of them to stay there—for how long? They were sitting side by side. But it seemed to her that at a café terrace, you normally sat facing each other. She saw him in profile, and suddenly that profile reminded her of someone. She had heard that people are often more recognizable in profile than head-on, and for once she trusted her memory. She'd end up discovering once and for all whose profile this was. And besides, there was the disturbing fact of being seated side by side, as if traveling in a train or a bus.

"What part of Paris do you live in?"

"I've always lived in the 15th arrondissement."

She wondered whether she hadn't met him at around the same time as the large brunet with the sheepskin jacket and the other one, the one who worked for a moving company. But she no longer knew their names. And anyway, was it really in the 15th arrondissement?

"The neighborhood has really changed . . ."

"Just the opposite of Rome. Here, nothing ever changes . . . This plaza has been like this forever . . ."

"Do you know the 15th arrondissement?"

He was looking her in the eye with odd insistence.

"I don't believe so."

"I could make you a list of everything that's changed there, in recent years . . ."

It wasn't only his profile, but also his gaze that reminded her of someone.

"They've knocked down all the buildings along the river . . . even the La Marine Dance Club . . ."

He shrugged and, in a lower voice, almost a whisper:

"And the post office on Rue de la Convention . . ."

He smiled. It was as if he'd just recited the end of a poem, a little like the refrain that Sancho Lefebvre repeated in another lifetime: "Brainos's castle in Sologne" . . .

Once again she felt as if she were traveling next to him in a railway compartment. Or rather, in a bus.

S he had walked him to his hotel, in a street that, from Piazza del Popolo, led to the Tiber.

"If you like, we could have dinner tomorrow."

"With pleasure."

"Meet me at the gallery, at the same time."

"I'll hold onto Gaspard of the Night's album."

She walked along Via Flaminia to head home. No one. She had no idea what time it was. If it was still running, she would gladly take the streetcar.

Fragments of recollections paraded by randomly, belonging to that same period in her life. A small house beneath the trees, next to Brainos's chateau in Sologne. In the ground-floor room with its dark woodwork, they had installed a pool table. Her room was one flight up. A man had come to meet her at the Vierzon train station, a certain Paul whom Sancho Lefebvre said was "gap-toothed." She had been reunited with Sancho Lefebvre in Brainos's chateau. And then, after a while, the two of them had gone off

by car. Sologne. Annecy. Switzerland. Rome. Or
else Annecy. The Cote d'Azur. Rome. She didn't
remember whether they had crossed the Italian border via Ventimiglia or Switzerland. Once
back in Rome, she had never again left the city.
The month of November when she had come
for the first time . . . It was raining. Up to Porta
Pinciana, the avenue was as dark and empty as a
seaside boardwalk that the summer tourists had
abandoned. But she repeated to herself a phrase
she had heard somewhere: *The fair season is near.*

It was the first time she had strained her memory so hard. And suddenly a veil tore, and still
older recollections slowly rose to the surface, related to a snowbound landscape, the landscape
of her childhood, well before she had changed
her name. She was no longer in Sancho Lefebvre's car being driven from Sologne to Italy,
but in a bus, one of those buses you caught at
Place de la Gare in Annecy. They were parked in
front of a building whose façade was disjointed
planks—a dilapidated hotel, like an old chalet,

that made her wonder who the clientele could possibly be.

Wintertime buses and summertime buses. In winter, you waited for them very early in the morning, and their headlamps cast a yellow light on the snow. From the village, they went all the way down to Annecy. They stopped at Place de la Gare, in front of the hotel. On the ground floor, a café was still open and a few customers were standing at the bar, the last customers of the night.

And the Sunday evening buses. From Annecy, they climbed up to the village, with several stops, and it seemed to her that those Sunday evenings were always in winter. Many more people in those buses. Often there were no free seats.

The summertime buses. She caught them in Place de la Gare, in Annecy, at around 6 p.m., after work. They skirted the lake via Avenue d'Albigny. Outside the window, she imagined a fragrance of holidays and suntan lotion. Past a long alley lined with tennis courts, you could see the

façade of the Hôtel Impérial that hid the beach.
But soon the bus turned left onto a sloping road
and headed far from the lake, deep inland. Each
time, at that very moment, she felt like fleeing.

She took those buses, in both summer and
winter, at the same times. With the same people.
She had noticed a boy her age. In summer, he
got on the 6 p.m. bus in Annecy and got off at
Veyrier-du-Lac, just before the bend in the road
that led inland. On Sunday evenings, he got on
at the Veyrier-du-Lac stop and got off, like her,
at the entrance to the village where she lived.

They were often seated on the rear bench,
side by side. One late afternoon, on one of the
summertime buses, they had fallen into conversation. She was returning home from work. But
what work did she do that summer? Server in a
pastry shop beneath the arcades? Hired with the
other girls at Zuccolo? At the time, she hadn't
yet changed her name.

In winter, on the Sunday evening bus, he was
heading back to boarding school. On those evenings, they stayed standing, squeezed against

each other for the entire trip. They parted company at the square in front of the town hall. A few times she had accompanied him along the small, narrow road that led to the school, and they both walked slowly so as not to skid on the snow. You never forget the passengers on those buses that you used to take in winter and summer. And if you think you've forgotten them, you need only find yourself with one of them someday, side by side, and observe their face in profile to bring it all back.

That's what she was telling herself earlier. And what about him, had he recognized her? She had no idea. Tomorrow, she'd be the first to speak. She would explain everything.

PATRICK MODIANO, winner of the 2014 Nobel Prize in Literature, was born in Boulogne-Billancourt, France, in 1945, and published his first novel, *La Place de l'Etoile,* in 1968. In 1978 he was awarded the Prix Goncourt for *Rue des Boutiques Obscures* (published in English as *Missing Person*), and in 1996 he received the Grand Prix National des Lettres for his body of work. Modiano's other writings in English translation include *Suspended Sentences, Pedigree: A Memoir, After the Circus, Paris Nocturne, Little Jewel, Sundays in August, Such Fine Boys, Sleep of Memory,* and *Family Record* (all published by Yale University Press), as well as the memoir *Dora Bruder,* the screenplay *Lacombe Lucien,* and the novels *So You Don't Get Lost in the Neighborhood, Young Once, In the Café of Lost Youth,* and *The Black Notebook.*

MARK POLIZZOTTI has translated more than fifty books from the French, including works by Gustave Flaubert, Marguerite Duras, Jean Echenoz, Raymond Roussel, and nine other volumes by Patrick Modiano. A Chevalier of the Ordre des Arts et des Lettres and the recipient of a 2016 American Academy of Arts and Letters Award for Literature, he is the author of eleven books, including *Revolution of the Mind: The Life of André Breton,* which was a finalist for the PEN/Martha Albrand Award for First Nonfiction; *Luis Buñuel's Los Olvidados; Bob Dylan: Highway 61 Revisited;* and *Sympathy for the Traitor: A Translation Manifesto.* His essays and reviews have appeared in the *New York Times,* the *New Republic,* the *Wall Street Journal, ARTnews,* the *Nation, Parnassus, Bookforum,* and elsewhere. He directs the publications program at The Metropolitan Museum of Art in New York.